LP
O
ADA

JY 11 17

A Partnership
with Death

Center Point
Large Print

Also by Clifton Adams and available from Center Point Large Print:

Biscuit-Shooter
Stranger in Town

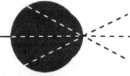

**This Large Print Book carries the
Seal of Approval of N.A.V.H.**

A Partnership with Death

CLIFTON ADAMS

CENTER POINT LARGE PRINT
THORNDIKE, MAINE

This Center Point Large Print edition
is published in the year 2017 by arrangement with
Golden West Literary Agency.

First US edition: Doubleday
First UK edition: Collins

The text of this Large Print edition is unabridged.
In other aspects, this book may vary
from the original edition.
Printed in the United States of America
on permanent paper.
Set in 16-point Times New Roman type.

ISBN: 978-1-68324-454-7 (hardcover)
ISBN: 978-1-68324-458-5 (paperback)

Library of Congress Cataloging-in-Publication Data

Names: Adams, Clifton, author.
Title: A partnership with death / Clifton Adams.
Description: Center Point Large Print edition. | Thorndike, Maine :
    Center Point Large Print, 2017.
Identifiers: LCCN 2017015294| ISBN 9781683244547 (hardcover : alk.
paper) | ISBN 9781683244585 (pbk. : alk. paper)
Subjects: LCSH: Large type books. | GSAFD: Western stories.
Classification: LCC PS3551.D34 P37 2017 | DDC 813/.54—dc23
LC record available at https://lccn.loc.gov/2017015294

A Partnership
with Death

Chapter One

For every man like Richter there was a town, somewhere, like Prosperidad. The place affected him like a woman of a certain sort. He detested it but he couldn't stay away from it.

From time to time he would find himself with a few hours or a few days on his hands, and he would tell himself that this time it would be different. He would tell himself that he would stay put and enjoy Don Antonio's hospitality and the fine Chihuahuan weather—even though it was February and the gritty wind cut through his canvas brush jacket like well-honed banderillas. Anything, he would tell himself, was better than Prosperidad.

He would remind himself of the saloon-keeper's daughter, always jolly and not too fat, in El Cuervo. And he had thoughtfully considered the various attractions of Ojinaga, or Ignacio, or Bosque Bonito, any of which was bigger and livelier than Prosperidad.

But here he was. In Prosperidad. It was a stinking, grubby little end-of-the-world place, maybe thirty dun-colored adobe huts huddled on a slope so rocky and barren that even Gila monsters and rattlesnakes avoided it. At the bottom of the slope there was a mud-hut saloon known as Maria's. For the sake of appearances Richter stopped here and took a beer with Maria, who stank of garlic and bad teeth and sweated-out tequila. The beer was warm and flat and going sour. The girls were fat and dirty and would happily slit your throat for the price of a pulque.

Despite the poisonous atmosphere of the place, Richter usually stopped here briefly, on his way to the square. To have ridden straight up to the crest of the slope would have been too obvious.

As if the whole town didn't know very well what had brought him to Prosperidad. Richter, and others like him.

From Maria's he made his way by convenient stages to the square, that part of town nearest the crest of the slope. His apparent goal was an establishment known by the strangely foreign name of Kopec's. But the real goal was some distance farther north—about twenty miles beyond the north bank of the Bravo.

Richter dismounted in front of Kopec's. He paused on the dirt walk, lighting a cigarrillo and staring with quiet fixity at those distant hazy ridges called the Chanattes. Then he spat into the street and went into Kopec's.

Kopec was behind the bar. He eyed Richter with a cautious grin. "Friends today, amigo?"

Richter shrugged. "Whatever you say."

Kopec laughed. "Friends, then. Tequila?"

Richter nodded and Kopec set out the bottle, the glass, and a box of salt. Richter drank Mex style, licking salt as he threw down the tequila. It wasn't that he liked salt with tequila, he just hated tequila more by itself.

"How's your head?" Kopec asked.

Richter shrugged and the barkeep laughed. "You was a curly wolf that night. Remember?"

"Not much." There had been a fuss and Kopec had laid Richter out with the heavy glass base of a coal-oil lamp. Richter had been out for almost two hours and had finally come to in the alley behind Kopec's cantina.

"You remember what that fuss was about?" Kopec asked.

"No."

"Me neither." He leaned on the bar and sighed contentedly. Kopec was a square-built, happy little bohunk with a shiny bald head and handsome black mustaches. Five years ago he had come across the Bravo on a cattle buying expedition in Prosperidad. There he had met and married the widow of Jesús Alverez, the original owner of the cantina. It was the perfect marriage. Señora Kopec, a dagger-sharp businesswoman, controlled the family purse strings in a way that would have been unthinkable had Alverez lived. As for Kopec, he had a place where he could drink with his friends, which was all he wanted.

Richter threw down another tequila. "I guess

you ain't seen anybody . . ." He made a vague gesture, indicating the distances beyond the doorway.

Kopec shook his head. "The one you're lookin' for ain't never comin' across the Bravo. Why don't you give it up, Richter?"

Richter looked at him, downed a third tequila, but said nothing.

The barkeep sighed and poured himself a shot from Richter's bottle. Such was the informality of the place. "New girl started work the other day, if you're interested."

"I ain't."

A bull buyer and one of Don Antonio's vaqueros came in and took a table with two girls. Kopec went to see what they wanted. Richter picked up the bottle and took it to a table near the front door. He sat for a long while looking out at the hazy mountains. His thoughts moved in a narrow, deceptively calm channel. Strange, the difference twenty miles could make. Somewhere out there an insignificant-looking, silted-up river separated two worlds. The world out there beyond those ridges had been his world . . . once. Now it was worth his life just to get close to it. Even sitting here in Kopec's was not safe, though it had never stopped him from coming here.

A woman was asking, "You care if I sit down?" She sounded as if she had asked two or three times before.

Richter stared at het without really seeing her. "What?"

"You care if I sit down?"

"You'll just be wastin' your time."

She shrugged, looked as if she might smile, but didn't. "It's my time. I've done worse things with it."

Richter was annoyed at having his thoughts interrupted. But he kicked out a chair and said, "If you want a drink you'll have to get a glass from Kopec."

He turned back to the mountains. The girl got a glass from the bar, came back to the table and took a chair across from Richter. She helped herself to the tequila. "You must be Richter," she said at last.

He turned toward her. It occurred to him for the first time that he had never seen her before. She must be the new girl that Kopec had mentioned.

He tried half-heartedly to guess her age and again experienced a kind of passing annoyance when he found that she might be pegged anywhere between twenty and forty. Her features were plain, undistinguished, and somehow blurred, like a photograph that had become faded from too much handling.

Her hair, if it had been washed, would have been chestnut, or maybe a shade lighter. Her eyes looked ageless and were a kind of slatey gray or blue. Obviously, Prosperidad was not her home.

11

Probably a border-town girl, Richter thought, that had followed some Mex sharpshooter south across the Bravo. Now the Mex was tired of her and she was trying to raise a stake to try her luck again in Texas. It was an old story.

He asked, "Why *must* I be Richter?"

The girl laughed, and it was a strangely disturbing sound, with no humor and very little life. "Everybody hears about Richter in Prosperidad. You're a famous man, don't you know that?"

As a matter of fact, Richter didn't know it—and he didn't like it. "What makes you say that?"

She shrugged with one shoulder, and it wasn't a bad-looking shoulder, as she well knew. She wore one of those gaudy blouses, the kind that Indian girls wore on saint days and fiesta—it showed off her shoulders. Around her neck she wore a small silver cross on a silver chain. Not that a crucifix meant anything in Mexico. Everybody wore them, even the men.

"Tell me how I got to be a famous man," he said. He dimly wondered if Kopec had been talking out of turn. It didn't sound like Kopec.

She poured herself another drink. "For one thing, you're in good with old Don Antonio. That makes you something special down here, even if there wasn't anything else."

"There's somethin' else?"

12

She looked at him steadily, as if she were trying to memorize his face. "You never figured to keep it a secret, did you? I mean, your trouble on the other side of the Bravo. What was his name? Udall? You killed one of his boys, and left Texas with four thousand in gold in your saddle pockets. So they say."

Four thousand! So that's what they were saying. He had known, of course, that some such yarn was going around, but he had never been interested enough to get the particulars.

"That makes me a pretty dangerous hombre," he said straight-faced.

The girl grinned fleetingly, showing him a bare hint of human feeling and warmth beneath her rice-powdered mask. "If you don't want to talk about it, it's all the same to me."

Richter said nothing. They sat for a while drinking tequila and licking salt. When the bottle was half empty, Richter paid Kopec for the drinks and went back into the street.

He was a big man, and when he walked into a room there was a certain awkwardness about him. Outside, he was lithe and animal-like, with a tendency to prowl instead of walk. Still in his thirties, there were significant streaks of gray in his dark hair. His eyes were pale, plainsman's eyes, and looked out of place here in the Mexican mountains. It had been almost a year since he had given any thought to his appearance. He washed and shaved whenever he happened to think about it, which wasn't often. He changed clothing when those he wore became too dirty for comfort. To look at him it was not easy to believe that, scarcely a year ago, he had been a rising Texas cowman. But that was before he had locked horns with Henry Udall.

He began to wish that the girl hadn't mentioned Udall; the memory of that name turned the tequila sour in his stomach.

He walked the street aimlessly. Dark eyes watched him from behind shuttered windows and darkened doorways. This, the looks said, was the man called Richter. Across the river there was a price on his head, so the story had it. But it would take a bold Mex to try for that bounty, as long as Richter stayed on the right side of Don Antonio.

He went to another cantina, but they didn't speak English there, and he didn't speak Mex, so he soon left. Strange how he seemed incapable of picking up the lingo. He was bright enough in other ways, but when somebody spoke Mex to him he simply stopped listening.

It was near sundown when he found himself heading for the old mud wall near the crest of the slope. It had been part of a corral once, long ago, but now this piece of wall was all that was left. Facing north, with your back to the wall, it was possible to shut out the racket of the town and, if you looked long enough and hard enough, those haze-blue ridges of Texas would seem to move toward you until you could almost reach out and touch them.

Richter didn't like this place, and he didn't like what the sight of those hills did to him. But more often than not, whenever he was in Prosperidad, he would come here for at least a little while. Come with the other exiles and look, and hope for the impossible, before going back to Kopec's and getting drunk.

It was a long-standing joke among the Mex citizenry of Prosperidad. At this very moment, Richter knew, some of them would be inching out into the dusty street, watching him expectantly, grinning. He knew what the good citizens of Prosperidad called this wall. They called it "the wailing wall."

Like many another exile, Richter suspected, he had come to this place the first time as a joke— now he couldn't make himself stay away. He had never given any thought to his homeland, until recently. Most of his life he had wandered from place to place; he couldn't remember ever being homesick, even as a kid. Now it ate at his bowels like a nest of worms.

But then, there were a lot of things whose existence he had never suspected until recently. For instance, it was only within the past year that he had developed a desire—almost a lust—for murder.

● ● ●

He lit a slender black cigarrillo and leaned against the wall and gazed out over twenty miles of desolation. He told himself that he didn't know when he was well off. Don Antonio was a first-class boss, and Richter knew that he was lucky to have landed a place with him. What had Texas or the Union ever done for him? The trouble with you, Richter, he thought to himself, is that you don't know when to let well enough alone.

It didn't do any good. The poison was in his blood, and there was no antidote. Except one—and that was beyond his reach.

In disgust he was about to start back to Kopec's when he saw the flash of gaudy color against the mud wall. There was no mistaking that blouse—the new girl from Kopec's was lounging in a niche in the wall, about twenty yards across the slope from Richter.

"How long you been there?" Richter demanded angrily.

She glanced at him undisturbed. "I was here before you came, if it makes any difference."

"How come I didn't see you?"

"How come you didn't look?"

Richter rubbed his jutting chin. "What're you doin' here?" he asked finally.

"Same as you. Lookin' and wishin'."

He scowled. "That your home range over there?" He nodded to the north.

"Yes."

"Texas?"

She hesitated, then nodded. "Yes."

"You in trouble with the law?"

The question seemed to puzzle her. "Why?"

"There's laws and laws. Some can be got around."

She startled him by throwing her head back and laughing—a harsh, jarring sound in the still afternoon. "No, the law doesn't want me."

He didn't understand her. That hunger in her eyes was unmistakable. Richter had seen the look of the exile too often. "If there ain't nothin' holdin' you," he said, "why don't you go home?"

She looked at him as if he were totally unique—as if she had never seen his like before. Then, without another word, she started walking back toward town.

Her manner disturbed him. There was still enough of the cavalier in Richter to know that she had been hurt. "If I said anything . . ." he started automatically.

"You didn't. It's time I went back to work."

"At Kopec's?"

She nodded.

At the moment he had nothing better to do, so he said, "I'll walk with you."

"No." She bit the word off sharply. "I mean, there's no need."

What did she mean by that? Richter wondered.

17

Did she think Richter was too grand to walk with her, because she worked the cantinas? He grunted and shrugged and put her out of his mind. He turned back to the north and finished smoking his cigarrillo.

This was a land of mountains and basins, violent geological contradictions. Here were great reaches of desertland, miles of gravel and sage and prickly pear and blackbush, all on a floor as flat as Kopec's beer; vast wastelands watched over by gigantic battlements of the Chisos, the Guadalupes, the Davis, and the Chanattes. There in the granite mountains grew the sotol, and lechuguilla. Cactus of a hundred insane varieties clung to towering stone walls. And on those perilous ridges, especially in the Guadalupes, there grew forests of pine and oak and cedar. In places the earth was red with copper, the hills oozed pure lead, the mountains were streaked with darkly glittering silver, and even gold. But the mining engineers had long since inspected this wild land and filed their gloomy reports—not fit for commercial mining.

The wealth of the land was not in silver or gold but in the austere grasses that thrived in tawny clumps and bunches on the gravelly floors of the various basins. This was rangeland, cattle-land.

It was one of nature's jokes. Cattle grow sleek and fat in the basins, but the region was an abomination to raisers of sheep and goats. Needlegrass, that ruiner of good wool and mohair, flourishes in the sand and gravel.

A cowman's dream. A country created for cattle and nothing but cattle. Richter knew. Once he had been a cowman there himself.

Directly south of the old wall there was a small, dusty plateau that passed in Prosperidad as the village square. Kopec's was on the south of the square, facing the Chanattes.

Richter hesitated in front of Kopec's adobe cantina. Lamps and candles of the town were being lit. An old woman was in the square cooking tacos on a charcoal brazier. In that rosy half light just before nightfall there was a kind of sad romance in the air.

"Comin' in?" The girl was looking at him from the doorway.

"In a minute." Richter crossed the square and bought six meat tacos from the old woman and brought them back in his hat. "Beer," he said to Kopec, and gestured for the girl to sit down. Kopec brought three warm, winey-tasting beers. The three of them sat in comfortable silence, eating and drinking. There were no other customers, just Kopec's two regular Mex girls who were playing cards at a corner table.

Kopec wiped his mouth with a flourish. "I got somethin' special," he said, and ducked behind the bar.

Richter drained his glass, looking at the girl. "You ain't sore?"

"Why should I be sore?"

Richter shrugged, recalling that quiet, belligerent toughness that had come over her at the wall. But she seemed all right now. Kopec appeared at the table with a bottle of golden rum and two glasses. He poured a dram for himself and one for Richter. Tacos and beer, all right, but aged rum was much too good for cantina girls.

Kopec sighed and smacked his lips. "Sweet as mothers' milk and honey!" He took the bottle back to its hiding place.

Richter called for tequila and began to drink. The February wind was gusty and cold, but the tequila was warming as it went down and Richter liked sitting by the open door. Even when it was too dark to see the mountains.

"You been here long?" he asked at last. If the girl was going to go on sitting there he felt obligated to say something.

"Four days."

"Where'd you come from?" Not that he cared.

"Cuervo."

"That's a pretty good ways." And that seemed to take care of that. "You want a drink?"

She nodded, and Richter had Kopec bring another glass. He was comfortable and beginning to feel the tequila, and he was satisfied to sit there doing nothing, not thinking, not speaking.

Kopec's was easily the class of Prosperidad cantinas. True, the floor was of swept dirt, and spiders and scorpions had a disturbing way of falling from the thatched roof into your food or drink, and the tequila would turn you blind after a time, if it didn't kill you outright. Still, Kopec's was the class of Prosperidad, and to be counted a Kopec regular was something of a local honor. Richter comfortably qualified as a regular. When he wasn't working Don Antonio's Piedras Negras bulls, or brawling, or secretly scouring the border towns for Udall men, he could usually be found at this table by the door.

Kopec sat down at the table. "A gringo horse buyer was in the other day from Bonito . . ." Bonito was a small international settlement about twenty miles from Glory, where Richter had once lived and worked. "Maybe you know this horse dealer," the barkeep went on. "Bird by the name of Cabot?"

Richter shook his head.

"Claimed to be an Army contract man. I never heard of an Army buyer rangin' this far south, though. Have you?"

"No. What was he interested in besides horses?"

Kopec looked vaguely worried. "Maybe nothin'. But it did seem like he perked up when I happened to mention Don Antonio's ganaderia."

Something about Richter seemed to slowly turn to stone. "Why didn't you mention this before?"

Kopec winced. "I just remembered."

"Could he have been a Udall man?"

"I don't know. A long, drawed-out galoot, wearin' a pony hide vest and a brush country hat, not much crown and even less brim. There was somethin' about the way he wore his .45—if you know what I mean."

Richter smiled thinly.

"You recollect anybody to fit that description?"

"No," Richter said, "but that don't mean anything. Udall hires his guns as he needs them."

"You reckon somethin' new's come up at Glory?"

Richter said nothing.

"Most likely it's nothin'," Kopec said.

A vaquero came in eating a tamale in a cornshuck and Kopec returned to the bar. Richter drank without relish, steadily but unhurriedly, as if he were quietly working out a system whereby one man, if he applied himself, might consume all the tequila in Chihuahua.

The girl said, "You drink this way often?"

Richter seemed surprised to find her still sitting across from him in the same chair. "Often as I get a chance," he said.

She helped herself to his tequila, throwing it down neatly and expertly, with a lick of salt. Kopec, looking as if he had been at the rum bottle again, came back to the table. "I figgered all along you'n Hessie'd hit it off." He gazed happily at Richter.

"Me and who?"

Kopec laughed. The girl said, "Jessie Marchand. In Mex it sounds like Hessie."

Richter, all but totally ignorant of the local lingo, failed to appreciate Kopec's small joke. He looked at the girl and said thoughtfully, "Marchand . . . Marchand . . ."

Kopec started to say something, but the girl stopped him with a look as black as the heart of a Piedras Negras bull.

"I know that name from somewheres."

"Plenty folks named Marchand," she said, reaching for the bottle.

"I never met one. No . . ." Richter shook his head. "It was somethin' I can't quite get hold of. It'll come to me."

They sat for a moment, Richter scowling in concentration, Jessie Marchand pale and motionless. Again Kopec started to speak and she kicked him savagely beneath the table.

"Marchand the gold hunter!" Richter said suddenly, pleased that he had finally thought of it. "That the one?"

Jessie poured herself a double tequila. "Yes."

"I remember now." His thoughts, with the aid of tequila, were soaring. "Marchand your husband?"

"Was," she said tonelessly.

"That's right. Got himself killed by Indians, didn't he? No," he corrected himself, "not Indians. Bandits." He looked suddenly puzzled. "Funny, I don't recollect a wife."

"Sure you do," Kopec rushed in. "Husband killed, the woman captured by the Pepe Groz bunch. Four, five months, and not a word. Then one day there she come, walkin' out of the Las Damas!"

"Sure, sure!" Richter was a little drunk, but not too drunk. Not as drunk as he would be before the night was over. He appreciated this diversion, this little mystery that surrounded the insignificant life of a cantina girl. It left him less time to think about his own problems. "That must of been a right smart trick," he said in genuine admiration. "Gettin' loose from a lobo like Pepe Groz."

"I had something they wanted," she said quietly. "We . . . did some trading."

Richter was confused. He scowled and drank a tequila. "Gold?" he said at last. "The way I heard it, there wasn't any gold."

Kopec laughed explosively and slapped Richter between the shoulders. "Not gold, amigo! No sir, it sure wasn't gold!" He got up and went to the bar, still laughing.

Richter stared. Little by little the truth was becoming apparent. Like an ocelot rising up in a dappled shade, at first it was only a confusion of spots and color. Then, little by little, the confusion took form.

Richter hadn't bothered to wonder where the conversation was leading them. It had started as a harmless diversion, something to relieve his boredom. But the path had taken an unexpected turn, and suddenly he found himself up to his chin in something ugly.

"Listen," he said suddenly, "I never knew anything about . . ."

"Forget it," she said, weary of the subject, sick of it. She looked at him without emotion. "Don't let it bother you, Richter. I'm used to it by now." She smiled crookedly and looked almost sorry for him. Then she got up, took a red shawl off a nail behind the bar, and walked out of the cantina.

Richter's face was blazing. Suddenly he lurched up from the table and slowly advanced on Kopec. The barkeep sighed and felt along the bottom bar shelf for a bung starter. "Richter," he said pleadingly.

"You sonofabitch," Richter said, "I ought to knock that bar to pieces with your head."

"Richter," Kopec cautioned again, taking a good hold on the bung starter.

"Why didn't you tell me who that girl was?"

"I did. Just a minute ago. Now cool down."

"You never told me she was the one that was took by Pepe Groz and his bunch of cutthroats."

"You never asked," Kopec evaded.

25

The two Mex girls at the card table saw how the scene was developing. They quietly disappeared, like shadows sliding out the back way.

Sweat was beading on Kopec's shiny bald head. "Richter, we ain't goin' to start wreckin' the place, are we?"

"I ought to of wrecked it months ago, and burned it."

Frustration had Kopec almost in tears. "Damnit, Richter, just try and listen to me!"

To the barkeep's amazement, Richter took himself in hand. He glared at Kopec for several seconds. Then, without warning, he wheeled and slammed out of the cantina.

Kopec, his hands trembling, poured a generous glass of rum from his private stock and downed it. "Crazy damn gringo!" For the good of his nerves he had another glass of rum before putting the bottle away.

Chapter Two

Richter's line was cattle. On the job he was a top hand and drew top pay, but he hadn't touched anything like a regular job in almost a year. He was not yet forty, and his chances of getting much older were not good, the way things were going.

That was Richter. At the moment he was leaning on the bar in a place called Paco's. Two young Mex pistoleros, dressed gringo style in California pants and hickory shirts, were watching him carefully without appearing to. Udall men? Maybe. They had the look about them.

Richter crooked a finger at the barkeep. "Tequila." That was one word of Mex that he could say. He would have gone to Kopec's, but he was still sore at Kopec about the business with the girl. He was also quite drunk. So drunk, in fact, that one of the young bravos at the bar had just about decided that he could take him.

Richter grinned and saluted them with his tequila. "Udall's pickin' his pistoleros a little green nowadays, ain't he?"

One of them, a slight young man with a gleaming gold front tooth, said something under his breath and spat on the dirt floor. His friend, slightly older and much cooler, watched

Richter from the corner of his eye and lit a black stogie.

The cool one nodded politely in Richter's direction and said something in Mex. Richter didn't hear him. He had the barkeep pour another tequila. Then he leaned arrogantly on the bar, almost wishing that they would try for their guns. It had been almost nine months since the last Udall man had tried it. That one had got himself killed in just such a situation as this; he had wrongly guessed that Richter was too drunk to fight.

Young Gold Tooth felt that he had been insulted. He was angry. He would have forced things to a boil, and he would have died then and there, where he stood, if his cool friend hadn't been there to calm him.

Richter laughed at them. "You boys," he said, "are just too green and ignorant for my taste. I don't feel much like killin' you today. Unless there ain't nothin' else will suit you . . ." Leisurely, he downed another tequila. "If you're lucky enough to get back to Glory, tell Udall it's always a mistake to send boys to do a man's work."

Gold Tooth had gone slightly pale. He understood enough English to know that he had been insulted. But the cool one merely studied the end of his stogie and said pleasantly, "We no understand Udall. Who is this man?"

Richter grinned. "Think about it. It'll come to you." He paid up and left.

For some time Richter sat on a rock in the barren square waiting for Gold Tooth and his crafty friend to make their play. But they didn't come out of Paco's.

Could he have been wrong about those two? Was he getting so spooky that every strange face he looked at had to be a Udall man?

His stomach burned from the tacos and too much tequila. He promised himself that he was going to lay off tequila. It only got him into trouble and it did nothing to solve his problems.

He got up from the rock and made a tour of the square, peering into the sullen little cantinas. They all reminded him of Maria's at the bottom of the slope. Finally, when his boredom was sharp enough, he went back to Kopec's.

Kopec studied him doubtfully. "No fightin', Richter. My old woman won't hear of any more busted furniture."

Richter raised both hands, as if someone were holding a pistol at his back. "No fightin'. That's a promise."

Richter's promises were good just as long as his repentant mood lasted. But Kopec set up a bottle and they had a drink to their fragile truce.

"Where'd the girl go?" Richter asked.

"Jessie?" Kopec shrugged. "*Quién sabe?*"

"She really the one that Pepe Groz took up in the Las Damas?"

"We're not goin' through that again, are we?"

"I was just thinkin'. It must of been pretty rotten for her."

"It's a rotten world, Richter. Why don't you go back to the ganaderia and help with the bulls?"

"I ain't in the mood for bulls. Down at Paco's I ran into a cool Mex kid and his pal with a gold tooth. Duded up in California pants and blue shirts, from the other side of the Bravo." He looked at Kopec expectantly.

The barkeep groaned. "I don't keep track of every firebrand that rides through. Give it up, Richter. You'll never even the score with Udall. You'll never get him on this side of the Bravo, and he ain't likely to let you cross over."

"Gold Tooth and his pal have got the smell of Udall men about them."

Kopec was silent for a moment. There was a chance, of course, that Richter was right. They wouldn't be the first ones that Udall had hired to bring back Richter's hide. "I'll send one of my girls down to Paco's and see what she can find out."

A few months ago Richter would have laughed at Kopec for worrying. He wasn't laughing now. It got to you after a while, knowing that any stranger might be your assassin.

Kopec sent one of his Mex girls down to

Paco's. She came back and said that the pair was no longer there. Paco didn't know anything about them, and neither did the girls.

"That's a big help," Richter said sourly. He went to a horse trader's at the bottom of the slope where, for the price of two pulques, he was allowed to sleep in a vacant stall.

Don Antonio Pedro Gonzáles Mendoza y Mendenez leaned on the barrera of the small practice ring watching Manolo work with a black calf. Manolo, age twelve, was the elder of Don Antonio's two sons, and the old man's eyes glistened with pride. The boy, wearing the traditional *traje corto* of the amateur torero, cited with a muleta. "Huh, toro! Huh! Huh!" The calf, almost a year old and as fast as a bullet, drove toward the rag. The boy, with the arrogance of an emperor, bent the animal around his body with a left-handed *natural*.

"*Ole!*" Don Antonio cried.

Richter, in patient boredom, leaned on the barrera beside Don Antonio. Juanito, age two, was perched on Richter's shoulders, squirming excitedly. Manolo turned with dainty precision, linking three passes before freeing the calf. Juanito screamed and beat his small hands together. Don Antonio was almost in tears of joy.

Even Richter, who was totally indifferent to the

subtleties of bullfighting, nodded his approval. One serious mistake on Manolo's part and a year-old Piedras Negras could have broken half the bones in the boy's body.

"That will do," Don Antonio said at last, when he had his emotions under control. "There will be other calves. Your tutor is waiting; there are sums to be learned."

Reluctantly, the boy allowed two vaqueros to haze the calf out of the ring. Graciously, Manolo accepted his father's praise. He grinned fleetingly at the squirming Juanito on Richter's shoulders, and then solemnly shook hands with Richter. "We are very pleased that you have returned to us, Señor Richter."

"Glad to be back, Manolo. But it's hard on the nerves."

The boy looked puzzled.

"You take too many chances," Richter told him. "A Piedras Negras ain't no milk-cow, you know."

The boy laughed, recognizing the compliment. Don Antonio said sternly, "Yes, far too many chances!" But his face glowed with pride. Manolo and Juanito were the fruit of his old age and he treasured them shamelessly. Scolding affectionately, he hauled Juanito from Richter's shoulders and sent the boys off with the tutor.

"My sons are very fond of you, Richter," the old man said seriously.

"They're good boys."

"You'd make a good father. Haven't you ever thought of getting married?"

Richter was mildly outraged by this suggestion but tried not to show it. "Everything in its time, they say."

Richter had been helping to move some four-year-olds to the small pastures where they would stay until they were finally shipped to the great plazas in Mexico. A servant had come to him that morning with the message that Don Antonio wanted to see him at the big house. Richter had arrived at the beginning of Manolo's *faena* and was still cloaked in grayish dust.

Walking their horses, they moved slowly toward the big house. Don Antonio talked idly of the Christmas corridas, and contract men, and death-driven toreros, and brave bulls; anything and everything but what was on his mind. This, Richter had learned, was the way of Mexican aristocracy. When Don Antonio felt the time was right, he would come out with it.

The house, with the walls and slit windows of a fortress, was huge. This was not the first time that Richter had been inside it, but the vastness of it still impressed him. They passed through richly furnished rooms where fragrant piñon fires had been laid. On the walls there were faded tapestries and darkly glowing portraits of old Spaniards, some in Conquistador armor.

Some of the massive, intricately carved furniture dated from the age of Cortez.

Ahead of their line of march silent servants scattered like darting shadows. Richter strolled over priceless Moroccan rugs, his spurs clamoring. He was impressed by the vast wealth and power and position that the house represented, but not overly impressed. The house, the bulls, the ganaderia, none of them touched him in a way that would permanently change his life in the slightest.

His position at the ganaderia was unique and privileged, a fact that he accepted with no fuss and very little surprise. There was no telling who would be touched when blind chance reached out her hand. One day he had been a common roustabout on the bull loading crew, the next he had been a person of great importance. That was the way chance worked. All women, as Richter knew them, were highly unreliable, but the lady called Luck was the most capricious of them all.

"*Fino*," Don Antonio said to one of the attentive shadows, and as if by magic there was a servant with glasses and a crystal decanter. Don Antonio poured a glass for Richter and one for himself. They saluted gravely and drank.

Richter, his sense of taste all but dead, the victim of raw tequila, drank the wine like water. Don Antonio, out of politeness, did the same.

That fine old wine with the golden sun of Jerez in it.

Don Antonio cleared his throat. The time to speak his mind had come. "Richter, in the City of Mexico I have an old and cherished friend, as dear to me as a brother. This friend, Señor Dominic, has appealed to me in his time of great difficulties . . ."

The old man was as transparent as the Venetian glass of the wine decanter. Richter grinned faintly. "This Señor Dominic wouldn't be a bull raiser, would he?"

"You know of him?" Don Antonio's eyes widened.

"No, but I can guess his difficulties. He's havin' trouble with his shippin' crew and he needs a man just like me to get him straightened out."

"How could you have known!"

Richter shrugged. "I can't go to Mexico City, Don Antonio."

Those old eyes saddened. "Not even as a favor to me?"

"Not even for that. Why do you want to get me out of Chihuahua?"

The old man looked stunned. "How can you ask such a question!"

"The lowest peon on your ganaderia knows more about fightin' bulls than I do. If Señor Dominic's havin' trouble, I'd be about the last man he'd want to straighten him out. I think you worked it out with him just to get me out of this end of Mexico."

Don Antonio sagged into a chair, defeated. "You know how much I am in your debt, Richter. Why won't you let me help you?"

"You don't owe me anything. It's the other way around, if you want the fact of the matter."

"I owe you for the life of my son."

"If I did anything to help the boy, it was because it was what I happened to want at the time. You can't owe me for a thing like that."

"Nevertheless . . ."

They had been over this before and it made Richter uncomfortable. He tried to haze Don Antonio back onto the track. "Has something come up that I don't know about?"

Don Antonio made a helpless gesture. "A man called Cabot."

Cabot. Richter searched back through a tequila haze. In Prosperidad, Kopec had mentioned a man by that name. "Gunslinger?" he asked.

"So it is believed." Don Antonio spoke to an invisible shadow on the other side of the doorway. Then in English, he said, "Angel Hernandez has some knowledge of the matter. He will come shortly and you may speak to him."

They had another glass of wine. Richter wandered about the room, which was as much a part of Don Antonio as his skin and bones. There was an entire wall of books. The virile fragrances of leather and wax and piñon and fine Spanish wine lay on the still air. The head of an enormous Piedras Negras bull was mounted over the fireplace, and below it crossed banderillas, and the red and gold colors of Don Antonio's ganaderia. It was an extravagantly rich room, and yet Richter felt at home here.

A vaquero, his sombrero clinched tightly in both fists, was shown into the room. Don Antonio said, "This is Angel Hernandez; I know him to be an honest man. He will tell you what he knows about the man Cabot."

Angel spoke in halting Spanish and Don Antonio translated. The man known as Cabot had been in the neighborhood for several days. He was neither a working man nor a gentleman; the Mexicans didn't know what to make of him, but they were vaguely disturbed by his presence. The Indian peons especially were upset and believed that Cabot had the evil eye.

"Aside from the evil eye, what does he look like?" Richter asked.

Cabot, Angel said, was tall, clean shaven, and thoroughly somber. He wore a small, strange-looking hat, and a leather vest with the hair left on. And, of course, he wore the inevitable single-action .45.

That was Kopec's man. Brush hat, pony hide vest, and all. Richter nodded and Don Antonio told the vaquero to continue.

Well, said Angel nervously, maybe it was nothing, but two days ago, when Richter had been with a fence-mending crew in the west pasture, the stranger had approached some vaqueros near headquarters. He had asked particularly for Richter. The vaqueros, not easily intimidated, told the stranger that it was not their business to know the whereabouts of Señor Richter. They also told him that he was trespassing on private property, and what was worse he was trespassing in a pasture of three-year-old bulls. As any fool knew, fighting bulls must have as little human contact as possible. Later some Indian laborers, frightened of the evil eye, told him that Richter was with the fence-mending crew.

Richter sat for a moment in thoughtful silence. Lady Luck had cast the dice for him and they had come up seven. In another pasture at that particular time, a young bull with a splintered horn had required his attention, and he had left the fence crew. Maybe it meant nothing, or maybe it meant that blind chance had cheated Cabot out of an easy kill.

Don Antonio and the vaquero were watching Richter expectantly. He shrugged. "Probably somebody I talked to in Prosperidad, lookin' for a job."

"Angel hasn't finished," Don Antonio said. He motioned to the vaquero.

Sometime that same afternoon, Angel continued, a peon on the fence crew happened to see the stranger on a slope overlooking the place where they were working. Later they saw him again in a different place, but, as before, watching the crew. Once he was on horseback, the other time he had been sitting on a rock, holding a rifle across his knees.

A cold wind seemed to drift through the room. "And then?" Richter asked.

The vaquero shrugged. And then nothing. Some vaqueros came to see how the workers were doing, and the stranger disappeared.

"Anybody seen him since then?"

Angel shook his head.

When the vaquero had gone back to his duties, Don Antonio said, "Now do you understand why I want to send you to Mexico City?"

"Yes. I'm obliged, but I still can't go."

"Is revenge so important to you, Richter?"

Richter fumbled for a black cigarrillo and lit it. "I don't know about revenge. I just know that I let Udall run me across the Bravo, but I can't let him run me clean off the map."

"Is getting yourself murdered going to help?"

Richter grinned. "Let's hope it don't come to that."

A servant appeared in the doorway and apologized for interrupting, but there was a local official of some importance asking for the *patrón* . . .

Don Antonio rose reluctantly. "Stay where you are, Richter. This won't take long."

Don Antonio was hardly out of the door when another servant entered with a bottle of tequila and a crystal dish of salt and some cut limes. Richter sniffed the bottle. This was not the clear, raw liquid fire that Kopec served; Don Antonio's tequila was golden mellow with age and oak cooperage. Richter squeezed some lime juice on his tongue, added a pinch of salt, then threw down half a glass of the amber tequila. The liquor warmed his heart like the memory of an old love. He had two more drinks before putting the bottle down.

Cabot needed some thinking on; there was not much question about that now. Until now Udall's gunmen had been young hotheads. Now he had sent a rifleman, a professional. That meant that Udall was getting down to business. It might also mean that Udall was getting a little nervous.

Richter thought back to the day in question, the day that Cabot had come hunting for him on his own ground. That was not like a professional killer. Professionals were careful; cautious. Assassins were great ones for empty spaces and no witnesses.

Don Antonio came back into the room. He looked at Richter and poured himself a glass of tequila. "I have been talking to an old friend—an official of the State Police."

Richter experienced a certain uneasiness. "About me?"

Don Antonio nodded. "You and the man Cabot. In villages rumors travel like the plague, but the police cannot afford to ignore them. They are saying now . . ." He took lime juice and salt and downed his tequila. "They are saying that you are a marked man. The police are nervous. They have many troubles of their own . . ."

Richter grinned faintly. "On top of everything else they don't want a murdered American on their hands."

The old man sighed. "The police would be much happier if you were not so close to the border. The officials feel that you make too tempting a target for your American enemies. You understand that personal wars cannot be allowed on an international frontier."

"They want me out of Chihuahua?"

"Out of Mexico altogether, preferably. But of course it would no longer be so much a problem if you were to move to Mexico City."

The writing on the wall was clear; his pleasant stay on Don Antonio's ganaderia was over. "How long do they give me to start traveling?"

Don Antonio shrugged sadly. "The police are rather anxious."

"I'll be gone tomorrow."

The old man brightened. "Excellent. I will give you a letter to my friend in Mexico City."

Richter had no intention of leaving Chihuahua, but he didn't say so. He smiled and they drank a tequila together, and Richter left.

He took the long way from Don Antonio's and it was late when he reached Prosperidad. He approached the town from a cactus thicket on the west slope. He didn't think anyone had seen him.

Most of the town was asleep, but there was still a light in Kopec's. That was something.

Four listless vaqueros were playing poker at one of the front tables. Kopec's two Mex girls had already gone home, or wherever it was they went to when their day was over. The new girl was sitting like some solemn statue at Richter's table by the open front door. Kopec, with a wide, wet smile, was pouring himself a glass of golden rum from his private bottle.

Richter picked up some gravel and lobbed it toward the bar from the back door of the cantina. Neither the girl nor the vaqueros noticed the small sound. Kopec cocked his head like a happy owl and downed his rum. But he didn't look so happy when he went to the door and saw Richter standing just beyond the slant of light.

"Whatever it is," the barkeep said quickly, "I don't want any part of it."

Richter pulled him out of the light. "What're you talkin' about?"

"The Mex police was here today, askin' about

you. I don't want nothin' to do with them. You ever see the inside of a Mex jail?"

"Askin' about me?" Richter hadn't expected them to start worrying so soon. "What'd they want to know?"

Kopec shrugged. "If I'd seen you. If you'd crossed back over the Bravo." The barkeep squinted into Richter's face. "You don't aim to go back, do you?"

Richter ignored the question. "They say why they was so interested?"

"Police're the same all over. They don't tell you anything, they just ask questions. But they was some Federales in here a while back and I heard 'em talkin'. The governments on both sides of the Bravo are workin' on a set of international agreements. The kind of thing that could mean big money to both sides, so the last thing anybody wants is border trouble."

Richter knew what that meant. If the police found he hadn't left the country they'd throw him into some stinking *calabozo* and lose the key, just to make sure he wouldn't embarrass anybody by getting himself killed. He said, "You seen any more of that hardcase in the pony hide vest?"

"Just the time I told you about."

"Don Antonio's Indians've got the notion he's out to drygulch me."

Kopec was silent for a moment. After a while he said, "Things must be boilin' over in Glory."

"That's what I've got to find out. I don't like the notion of walkin' into a crossfire without even knowin' what it's all about."

But getting information out of Glory would be about as easy as stealing money right out of Udall's pocket. Udall jealously guarded what was his. And Glory was his.

"There's a hide and tallow man," Kopec said slowly. "Works both sides of the river. Everybody knows him. Might be, if we could get him to keep his ears open . . ."

Richter was instantly alert. "How soon'll he be goin' back across?"

"Two, three days. He's down at Paco's place. Paco's his brother-in-law."

"If you and him are pals, maybe he'd do some listenin' for us when he gets to Glory."

Kopec snorted. "Hide and tallow men don't have pals."

Richter rubbed a hand over his face. He could feel opportunity slipping through his fingers. "If it's money he wants, I ain't got much, but . . ."

"It ain't money."

There was something in Kopec's tone that rubbed strangely on Richter's nerves. "What is it, then?"

"Jessie. He took a real shine to her."

Only after a moment's thought did Richter recall that Jessie was Kopec's new girl. "If he took a shine to her, what's he doin' down at Paco's?"

Kopec shook his head in wonder. "Richter, it might be that you know somethin' about cows, but you've got a lot to learn about women. There's cantina girls and cantina girls. It takes an old hand to do business with a hide and tallow man."

Richter felt his face burning. Not many nights ago he had been sore at Kopec for his ungentlemanlylike ways.

Kopec laughed. "Might be you could talk reason to her. She likes you. I saw that much the last time you was here."

"I'll think of somethin' else," Richter said coldly. "Bring me a bottle of tequila."

He went off a little way from Kopec's and sat on the running gear of a derelict wagon. A darkness blacker than the night closed around him.

Suddenly he looked up and the girl, Jessie, was standing beside him with a bottle and a glass in her hands. "Kopec said you wanted this."

He took the bottle and glass and nodded. "All right. I'll pay Kopec later."

"Kopec said there was something else you wanted." She sounded puzzled.

"Kopec was wrong," Richter said. But when she did not return to the cantina, he said, "Sit down, if you want to. We can drink out of the same glass." He had the feeling that it would be better if, at this particular moment, he were not left alone.

She stood for a moment with a puzzled air and then sat near him on the wagon tongue. She wore the same gaudy blouse that he had seen before, or one just like it. She wore the red shawl over her head and hugged it around her shoulders.

Richter filled the glass and they shared it. A few months ago Richter would have said that drinking Kopec's kind of tequila without lime juice or salt would have been impossible. But it could be done. It depended on how much you wanted the drink.

"What did Kopec tell you?" he asked at last.

"Nothing. Just to bring the bottle."

It was in his mind to ask her to go to the hide and tallow man and get him to find out what was going on in Glory. But then he looked at her, and a shelf of clouds passed from under the moon, and she looked so thoroughly tired and disgusted with life that he couldn't do it.

"What is it?" she asked. "Is anything wrong?"

"Everything's fine," he said wryly.

"No." She shook her head. "Something's wrong. Is it something I could help with?"

This was the perfect time. Kopec was right. She did like him. He could see it now, and hear it in her voice. He said, "Why would you want to help me?"

She shrugged, pulling the shawl tighter about her shoulders. "I don't know. Because you treat me the way you'd treat any other woman, I guess."

"Is that so much?"

"If you're a woman and if you'd been five months in the mountains with Pepe Groz, it is."

He could think of nothing to say to that. They had another drink of tequila. She took it like medicine, shuddering, but she never refused a drink when it was offered. She looked at him in a curious way, and he said, "What do you see?"

"I was wondering about you and Don Antonio."

Richter laughed. "A lot of folks wonder about that. What's a big hidalgo like Don Antonio doin' knockin' around with a Yankee saddle tramp? There's no big mystery about it. Once I happened to be at the right place at the right time and snatched one of his kids from under a bull."

But it hadn't been all that simple.

Juanito had been riding behind the cantle of his father's saddle. It was not in Don Antonio to refuse his sons anything, and the boy had wanted to see the loading of the bulls. A snake spooked Don Antonio's horse, and the next thing they knew Juanito was on the ground, beneath the hoofs of a ton of black death.

Richter did not even remember leaving his own animal. The vaqueros were yelling, and Don Antonio was completely paralyzed. The bull was just discovering the boy on the ground. More than once Richter had seen those great bulls lift full-grown horses on their horns and toss them over their backs.

Richter had jerked off his hat and slapped it in the bull's face. That is what he would have done if it had been a common range cow, itself not the gentlest animal in the world. At the time he hadn't really known enough about fighting bulls to be afraid.

But he learned. The bull forgot Juanito and gave Richter its whole attention. It charged with the speed of a puma. Richter felt a slight tearing sensation along his thigh and was stunned to see his leg instantly red. It was nothing, just a nick. Toreros got worse all the time and didn't let it bother them. A first-class matador would have finished his *faena* and made his kill and then taken maybe two or three turns of the ring before noticing such an insignificant scratch. A "scratch" to a good torero was anything but a groin wound or any other wound that didn't kill him outright. Richter did not take a laid-open thigh so calmly; he bellowed shamelessly for help, and the vaqueros rushed in with pikes and prod poles.

The boy was unhurt, but the bull was butchered and the meat distributed among the peons. A Piedras Negras was no fool. He had learned what it was to charge a dismounted man and draw blood. In a formal corrida he would ignore the cape and go immediately for the torero.

That was the way it had been. A brief incident of no importance, except to those involved. In bad weather Richter's thigh still ached, but he willingly accepted this small discomfort. It had made a great difference in his life, suddenly becoming the personal favorite of a man like Don Antonio. It was not likely that he could have remained so near the border for so long if it had not been for Don Antonio's patronage.

Richter and the girl sat in a weary, emotionless silence. After a while the poker game broke up in the cantina. Kopec appeared at the back door and came toward them.

"I'm closin' the doors now. Have you asked her?"

"No," Richter said with an edge. "There's other ways."

The girl looked from one to the other.

Kopec snorted. "Well, it's your business. But if I was in your boots I'd want to know what Udall was up to. You want to keep the bottle?"

"Yes," Richter said. "I'll pay you tomorrow."

"If you're alive tomorrow." Kopec went back to the cantina and closed the door and shutters and blew out the lamps. They heard him lock the front door and head toward the square.

"What were you going to ask me?" the girl asked.

"Nothin'. Forget it." He got to his feet. "I think I'll turn in." He had just decided that the next day he would ride for the international settlement at Bonito and see what he could find out. Jessie

Marchand still sat woodenly on the wagon tongue. "Well, good night."

"Good night."

He felt sorry for her and wished that he had never heard about the business with Pepe Groz. "I'd walk with you to where you live," he said, "but I'd just as soon not be caught on the street tonight."

"That's all right."

She watched him walk off toward the lower end of the slope, leading his horse with one hand and carrying the tequila in the other. Soon the night swallowed him.

Chapter Three

The horse trader had gone to bed, but Richter spread some clean straw in a vacant stall and stretched out. He had a drink of tequila and began to think about Emily. He started to take another drink when he heard the slight movement outside the stall.

Cabot? Maybe. How a killing was done was not so important to an assassin. The kind of chances he took usually depended on how much he had been paid. And Udall, when he meant business, did not pinch pennies.

Richter reached slowly for his revolver. He was fully clothed, but his rifle was at the foot of the stall with his riding gear. Well, he consoled himself, it wasn't a job for a rifle, anyway, at what promised to be point-blank range. It wasn't such consolation.

Now he had the .45 ready but did not want to give himself away by thumbing back the hammer. He found himself wishing for a different weapon altogether, one not so noisy. He lay very still. In the next stall a mouse was nibbling at a stray kernel of corn. In Richter's ears it sounded like the cracking of large bones.

Now he heard the movement again from beyond the stall gate. Someone was coming up on him very quietly and with infinite caution. Richter decided definitely that it was Cabot. This was a man of great patience, and assassins were nothing if not patient.

Did the stall gate move just the least bit, or was the poor light playing tricks with his eyes? Outside in the dobe corral horses huffed nervously. Richter waited. He could hear his own heart beating. It didn't seem much faster than usual.

Now the stall gate was moving, definitely. There was a bare suggestion of a hint of a sound as the latch was let off and the leather hinges took the weight of the gate. It was hard to believe that the gate of a ramshackle Mex horse stall could move so silently.

Suddenly the gate was thrown back, hard. A dark figure stood at Richter's feet, slightly crouching, one arm raised over its head. It wasn't Cabot. How he knew, he couldn't say—maybe it was the aura of hate that seemed to radiate from this tense, dark figure. Cabot the professional would keep it impersonal; he would be cold, silent, and efficient.

This surprise caused him to hesitate for just an instant. Nations could fall, history could reverse itself. In an instant. Or a knife could be thrown.

Richter glimpsed the sleek metallic gleam in the man's upraised hand. Even before he had thumbed and triggered the revolver, he knew it was too late. The knife was loosed and flying, and he went slightly sick, knowing what to expect.

Between the dobe stall partitions the .45 sounded like a brass Napoleon. The muzzle flash spouted almost in the man's face. Richter had his second surprise, before the flying steel bird nested in his shoulder. It was a dark, smooth, young face. It was an angry, hate-filled face, the dark eyes glittering in a fine tequila rage. His upper lip was curled in what must have been a perpetual sneer, revealing one gleaming gold tooth in front. And Richter found himself thinking idiotically, It sure took you long enough to get around to it! Then the steel bird landed, and bit deep.

Gold Tooth flew back from the stall gate, danced a graceless pirouette, spewing blood, and fell into a manure pile.

Richter, for the moment, put Gold Tooth out of his mind. He heard muffled thud of steel on bone as the knife imbedded itself in his shoulder. There was little pain at first, but a sheet of sickness pulled around his brain. He fought it off as he would have fought off a badger. There were men, he had heard, who had no fear of knives. Richter was not one of them. He had known bullets, and he had even known Comanche war arrows that had been dipped in rotten buffalo liver, but he hated and feared knives more than any other weapon.

But he knew what he had to do. Get the blade out, fast, before the pain started. If he waited, he might not have the nerve to touch it. He took the haft in his right hand and pulled with all his might. Pulled straight out and prayed that no important artery had been severed or bone damaged. Prayed that no ligaments had been cut and that the blade had been reasonably clean. Praying and cursing and mouthing idiocies, he wrenched the knife free.

This time no amount of fighting could hold back that hated sensation of falling. He plunged like a burnt-out star into a pit without a bottom.

But in some obscure corner of his mind a spark of reason warned him that unconsciousness was a luxury that he could not afford. He clawed his way back from the edge. He heard himself saying, "I got to get out of here. Me with a gun in my hand and a dead Mex in the manure pile. That's just what the police need. Take them about five minutes to get together a firin' squad. A hundred Don Antonios couldn't help me . . ."

He hauled himself to his feet and clung to the stall gate until the first wave of nausea passed. He tried to think. Up and down the slope lights were appearing behind shuttered windows. He thought of Kopec. Kopec was the only person he could think of who might conceivably be willing to help him. The ganaderia was too far, and anyway he didn't want to take this kind of trouble to Don

Antonio. It had to be Kopec. A place to lay low for a few hours, or maybe a day, until he could get himself organized.

Instinctively he reached for his rifle and found his saddle and bridle on the stall peg. *His horse!* If somebody found the animal here they would know that he had been here. He stumbled into the corral, lowered the pole gate and drove the big roan out of the enclosure.

All right, he thought. That took care of the horse. It was a present of Don Antonio's, so it would head directly back to the ganaderia. It left him afoot, but that was better than having an animal around that would likely get him shot.

It also left him with his riding gear. He should have sent it home with the horse, but it was a little late to think about that. Besides, it would have taken him half the night to get the animal saddled, the shape his arm was in. There was nothing for it, he would have to pack the saddle with him.

He gathered up his saddle, bridle, blanket roll, and rifle, which, altogether, came to about sixty pounds. "Fine," he muttered bitterly, "that's just what I need, sixty pounds of plunder to pack."

He had seen Kopec's house but he wasn't sure that he could find it in the dark. He wasn't even sure that he could make it to the square. A dazzling pain came to life in the area of his shoulder socket. There was some blood, but not a lot of it. He held his arm close to his side so that his clothing would soak up most of the blood. He didn't want it to dribble along the ground and leave a trail.

He climbed the slope behind the town, the way he had come the first time. He stepped very carefully because he was afraid that if he ever fell beneath his load he would never get up. He kept telling himself that just one knife wound in the shoulder shouldn't be taking this much out of him. But that didn't make the climb any easier. A knife in the bone was not something that you simply tied up with a bandanna and forgot about.

But he saw nobody on the street. Windows where lights had appeared after the pistol shot were beginning to go dark again. Mexicans, if given choice, tended to mind their own business; that at least was one thing about the country that Richter approved of.

At last he made it to the square. He could almost believe that he could see the pain radiating like heat waves from his bloody shoulder. Blood drummed in his ears and he felt that he was losing his hold on the saddle. But he got across the square. He stumbled half blind along those rocky, deep-rutted alleys that Prosperidad passed off as streets.

All the dobe huts near the square were as alike as a collection of cigar cans, but he recalled that Kopec's place did have a mud wall in front of it.

And a vine of some sort. He found a place that looked right. A dog rumbled threateningly from the darkness. Richter ignored it. He rattled the front window shutters.

"Kopec!"

A rangy dun colored dog—part wolf, he looked like—came out of the shadows, fangs bared.

"Kopec!"

Somebody inside the hut shouted Mex at the dog. It wasn't Kopec. Richter backed up slowly, his riding gear hanging against the gate as he hurried his retreat. What an ironic thing it would be to have everything ended, after almost a year, by a half-starved dog.

He paused and rested a moment against the wall. Which way? he wondered anxiously. Where had he taken a wrong turn?

He started back across the square, and then he saw the place and knew that this one was Kopec's. He rattled the shutters.

"Kopec!"

He heard some fast, excited jabbering on the inside. Soon Kopec appeared in the doorway looking like some angry, bald-headed ghost in his long gray nightshirt.

"You out of your head?" the saloonkeeper demanded. "Or just drunk? You know that my old woman don't allow . . ." Then he sensed that something serious was wrong. He came outside and whistled under his breath when he saw the bloody shoulder and the deathly pallor of Richter's face. "What you got yourself into, Richter?"

"Gold Tooth caught me with a pigsticker. I could use a little help, Kopec."

Kopec had long since forgotten all about Gold Tooth and his cool-headed friend. "Richter," he said matter-of-factly, "I like you fine long's you don't bust up my cantina or get the law to plaguin' me. But I can't help you. My old woman'd have my hide if I brought you in and let you bleed all over her puncheon floor."

Richter stared at him emptily. He looked in such poor shape that Kopec said, "I'm sorry, Richter, but I just can't . . ."

"It's all right." Richter was too tired and sick to be angry or even disappointed. He didn't have the most remote notion where he could go from here. He had even sent his horse away.

Kopec clawed at his bald head and cursed. "Didn't I hear a pistol shot not long ago?"

Richter nodded. "That was me shootin' Gold Tooth."

"How bad?"

"He was in a manure pile, down at the horse trader's, last I seen of him. He looked dead."

This time Kopec cursed with real feeling. "Maybe I could get you a horse to go with that saddle. That's all I can do for you."

"I don't think I can ride. Not long enough to do

any good." Then, with infinite weariness, he said, "It was just a notion. I never thought how much trouble I might be to a family man."

"Goddamnit, Richter!" Kopec said helplessly.

Richter grinned a watery grin. "It's all right, Kopec. I better get goin' now."

"Goin' where?"

"I'll set down somewheres and think about it."

He would sit down somewhere and pass out, and in the morning the State Police would grab him. And that would be the end of it.

"Wait a minute," Kopec said. "There's Jessie."

Richter stared at him with glassy eyes.

"The girl you was talkin' with behind the cantina."

"Oh." He just barely remembered the conversation.

From inside the dobe hut a stern female voice called something in Mex. "Look," Kopec said hurriedly, "it ain't far from here. A dobe place settin' by itself on the north of the square. It's the house that used to go with the old corral. You think you can find it?"

"Sure. But won't somebody be there?"

"The girl will be there. Jessie Marchand."

"I mean, won't somebody be with her?"

Now Kopec understood him. "No, she pays for the place herself and stays there by herself. I told you once, there's all kinds of cantina girls."

"What makes you think she'll take me in?"

"I don't think anything. But if she don't, you're in a bad way, amigo. Now I got to go back in the house." He hesitated for a moment, looking doubtfully at Richter. Then he shrugged and disappeared through the doorway.

The north side of the square. It might have been the dark side of the moon.

But he started, grimly placing one foot in front of the other. Somehow he gained the road. He went on putting one foot in front of the other. After what seemed a long time he stopped and cursed himself savagely for not turning the riding gear over to Kopec to keep for him. That was the least Kopec could do, it seemed, considering all the money Richter had spent in his cantina.

But he couldn't bring himself to turn back. He had to keep going the way he was headed or he would never get anywhere at all.

A place near the old mud wall. He found it finally, a sorry little cube of a hut huddled behind a small forest of dead weeds. He felt that his energies had been measured out to the last precise drop. This had to be the place. He had left no margin for error in the matter.

He rattled the shutter weakly and leaned against the dobe wall and almost went to his knees. His stomach began to roll. He felt that he was going to be sick. That would be a fine way to start the interview with Jessie Marchand. If Jessie

Marchand ever got around to answering the door. He rattled the shutters again.

He heard a stirring inside the dobe hut. "Who is it?"

It was the girl. Richter steadied himself. "It's me," he croaked. "Richter."

A lamp was lighted. The door opened and the girl, Jessie Marchand, stood backlighted in the doorway, swathed from chin to ankles in a colorless wrapper. She took one look at Richter and said, "Come in, quick."

Richter fell through the doorway. The girl grabbed him, broke his frozen grip on his rifle and riding gear, and eased him toward the bed. The bed was a pole bunk with a shuck mattress, but to Richter it was as soft as a fogbank. The girl only glanced at his bloodied shoulder.

"Bullet?"

"Knife," Richter said through his teeth. "It don't amount to much. It's mostly in my head. But the point stuck in the bone, and . . . I hate knives."

"I know," the girl said. "So do I." Never a word about what had happened or what he was doing here. He closed his eyes and fought off sickness and tried not to think about edged steel. "I'd be the last one to claim that gettin' shot was any fun," he heard himself explaining, "but there's somethin' about knives."

She said, "Here. Take some of this."

Richter opened his eyes and was not surprised to see that she was offering him a glass of tequila. Somehow he had guessed that Jessie Marchand was the kind of woman who would keep tequila.

He gulped it down and lay back on the rattling mattress and sighed. She filled the glass and he downed that too, and then he lay in a kind of mental grayness while the fire of the mescal thawed the ice in his gut.

The girl neatly cut the sleeve out of his shirt and brush jacket without moving his arm. She washed the wound with warm water and strong lye soap—that was all she knew to do. She had no medicine and doubted that there was any in Prosperidad. Carefully, she worked his feet out of his tight-fitting boots. She turned and saw that Richter was looking at her in a strange way.

"What is it?"

Richter had been looking at her all along but was actually seeing her for the first time. Without the rice powder mask and gaudy blouse she looked like a different woman. And her hair was let down, framing her face. Richter did not think of her as either homely or pretty, but merely as a woman who looked a little more than her age, a woman with a gentle touch.

She gave him a third glass of tequila and asked again, "What is it?"

"I'm sorry about Pepe Groz," he said. The knife

wound, and now the tequila, had made him light-headed.

The color left her face, but she only shrugged. "That was a long time ago. You better get some rest."

He felt dull and heavy. He knew that he had only to close his eyes and he would sleep. But first he had to let her know what she was letting herself in for.

"Look, there's a young Mex pistolero down at the horse trader's. I shot him. I think he's dead."

She nodded. "I thought maybe it was something like that."

It was in his mind to explain to her that his being here might well mean trouble to her. But she was an old hand at trouble.

When he awoke the next morning the girl was gone. He felt clammy and weak and empty-gutted. His shoulder felt as if it had been spiked to the mattress.

He found his revolver on the bed near his right hand. His rifle was propped against the wall within easy reach. The girl, wherever she had gone, had at least left him in a way to defend himself. She hadn't had second thoughts during the night and decided that being a good Samaritan wasn't all it was cracked up to be and started looking for the police. She had even left the tequila on the floor next to the bunk, but for the moment Richter let it alone. It occurred to him that during the past year he had leaned a good deal on the comfort of tequila. Maybe it was time he tried to stand alone.

The door opened and the girl entered with some things in a basket. She put them on the table near the fireplace—something in a bottle, three eggs, some freshly cooked tortillas, and a bloody piece of beef liver. "Here," she said, filling a glass from the bottle.

Richter looked at it and licked his cracked lips. "I figgered maybe I better slack off on drinkin', seein' the fix I'm in."

"Drink it," she said impatiently, and began chopping the liver and putting it into an iron pot. She chopped two onions and added them to the pot with some suet, and then she threw in some salt, a clove of garlic, and a peeled chili. Richter stared bleakly as she put the pot on a hook and swung it over the fire.

"What's that?"

"Liver hash," she said. "I can't do anything about your shoulder. You'll have to do it yourself, and you can't do it without food." She handed him the glass. "Drink," she ordered.

Richter tasted the murky liquid. It was pulque, the cactus brew that tequila was distilled from. It tasted faintly like soured milk; the peons were great believers in the healing qualities of pulque.

Richter drained the glass at a gulp. The girl

was busy at the fireplace, crushing coffee beans and putting them on to boil. She rendered a small piece of suet in a skillet, added the eggs and scrambled them.

"You won't believe it," she said soberly, "but I was a good cook once." She stood motionless for just a moment, her back to Richter. "I was a lot of things . . . once." She served the eggs in the skillet and she and Richter scooped them in tortillas and ate them. With some food in his belly, Richter was surprised at how much better he felt. He started to sit up in bed.

The girl said, "What do you think you're doin'?"

"I'm in better shape now. It's just the way I am about knives. I make it out worse than it is."

"Don't talk like a fool," she said flatly. "Set foot out of doors and you'll wind up in front of a firing squad. The State Police have already found that Mexican."

"Gold Tooth?"

She nodded. "He's dead. And so'll you be if you let yourself be seen."

Richter didn't like the sound of that. "They can't already know I killed him," he said doubtfully.

"I don't know about the police. But Juan Gomez knows. Remember the trouble you had with that pair down at Paco's? Juan Gomez is the quiet one."

Richter breathed deeply. So the cool one's name was Juan Gomez. Somehow Juan Gomez troubled him more at the moment than the police did. "I remember," Richter said. They had been opposites, one wild and one quiet, but somehow they had gone together. Like oil and vinegar, salt and pepper. Killing one of them was like killing one of a pair of snakes; you had to wait around and kill the second one or you'd never get any rest. "How does this Juan Gomez know so much?" he asked.

"He and his pal, Pablo, the one you call Gold Tooth, was down at Paco's last night. Pablo had made a trip to the outhouse behind the cantina. That was the last Juan saw of him. He figures that his pal must have seen you, probably as you went from Kopec's to the horse trader's place. Then, when Pablo caught you there in the horse lot, you shot him."

And that must have been just the way it had happened, Richter thought to himself. Still, it was only guessing on the part of Juan Gomez. The police would need more than that to go on. The girl asked, "Does anybody else know you were in Prosperidad last night?"

"Just Kopec."

"And Kopec's wife?"

Richter nodded. He had almost forgotten that Kopec was married.

"Can Kopec keep her quiet?"

"For a while," he said without much conviction. "Last night Kopec said something about gettin' me a horse. I'll be pullin' out before she gets a chance to do much damage."

"Do you have a place to go?"

Richter grinned weakly. Was there a country that would accept him where either assassins or police, or vendetta-bent pistoleros, wouldn't try to kill him? He couldn't think of one at the moment. "Sure," he said. "There's nothin' to worry about." Then he looked closer at the girl, Jessie Marchand. "What about you? You don't *have* to stay here, do you?"

She took the coffee off the fire and poured some into a cup and mixed it with pulque and gave it to Richter. She didn't look at him directly. For a while Richter thought that she was going to ignore the question completely.

"When I escaped from the bandits," she said at last, "not even the Indians or peons would have anything to do with me. In places where there is a lot of leprosy, I've heard, the lepers keep a bell with them and ring it whenever they go out, to warn others to keep away from them. That was the way I felt. Wherever I went a kind of silent bell began to ring. Somehow, as I came down out of the Las Damas, the word traveled ahead of me. 'Here is Pepe Groz's woman. It is worth a man's life to look at her. To touch her, a man could cook all day over a slow fire.' I almost starved before I found a priest to take me in and feed me."

She gave Richter the coffee and pulque. Then she sat in the crude, peasant-made chair beside the bed, and folded her hands in her lap, looking at Richter with an absence of expression, looking at him but not really seeing him.

"The priest," she said suddenly, "gave me something to eat and put salve on the cuts and scratches I'd got coming down out of the mountains, and finally he got one of the local farmers to take me north with him in a load of hay. That was how I got to Coyame. At Coyame another priest and some sisters took me in. The Coyame authorities came and I told them my story. I didn't have any folks of my own; my family died out in Louisiana ten years ago during a spell of fever. But Frank—my husband— Frank's people lived in Texas. A place called Sorano; maybe you know it."

Richter shook his head. He didn't really want to hear all these details, but now that she had started, he could think of no decent way to stop her.

"There's nothing special about Sorano," she said, picturing the place in her mind. "Black dirt. A little place not far from the Louisiana line, a town that fills up with farmers on Saturday and for the next six days is empty. The kind of town where one man usually runs everything—the bank, the biggest store, the church. You know what I mean?"

Richter nodded. In Glory his name was Udall.

"In Sorano," the girl said, "the man is Max Marchand. Frank's father. He runs everything in Sorano, and while Frank was there he ran him too."

She frowned with the effort of remembering. Frank had been dead just six months, but she could hardly remember what he had looked like—so much had happened since then. He had been a plain man; she remembered him only as a grayish shape of no particular distinction. But he had been kind, and foolish, and he had loved her. Jessie Marchand dwelled for a moment on that word. She supposed that she had loved Frank too, though the word had long since lost its meaning to her.

The bone-deep pain in his shoulder caused Richter to squirm. He could guess what was coming, and he didn't want to hear it. But the girl seemed to have a need to tell it, and the least he could do was listen.

"In Sorano," she said, "Frank was a little man, always in his father's shadow. He used to talk of leaving Sorano and striking out on his own, but nobody believed him. I didn't believe him. Then one day some prospectors passed through Sorano talking about gold. Across the Bravo, they said, men were striking it rich every day. The way they told it, gold was fairly oozing out of those mountains. But they didn't tell about the Indians in those mountains, who knew more about torture than the Comanches or Kiowas ever dreamed of. Or the bandit gangs who could have taught the Indians. They never mentioned the wildness and terrible lonesomeness of those mountains. . . ." She looked at Richter and smiled crookedly. "Prospectors never think about such things, I guess. Until it's too late."

"Frank—your husband—he got the gold fever?"

She nodded. "It was like a sickness came over him. He couldn't think or talk about anything else. Gold. He could see himself coming back to Sorano with a packtrain loaded down with it. Maybe then people would look to him instead of his father. He bought a pair of mules and began outfitting for the trip—not even threats and commands from his father could stop him."

Richter had known men with the gold fever, and it was pretty much as she had said. "I can understand about your husband," he said, not really interested, his mind on the pain in his shoulder. "But I don't see why he took you along. Didn't he know how bad it would be for a woman?"

She smiled again, that queer smile. "In Frank's mind there was gold, and that was all. He thought that if I was there to look after the camp and do the cooking and such, it would give him that much more time to dig the gold out of those mountains, and the quicker he could come back to Sorano a rich man."

The rest of it was a well-known story. They had blundered about from one rock-strewn wilderness to another, their supplies running low, escaping torture and death by sheer luck. And finally, in those ragged heights around Coyame, their luck had run out. They had stumbled onto the bandit gang led by Pepe Groz.

For the amusement of his bandits, Pepe had ordered Frank Marchand hung head-down over a bed of live coals. Marchand died slowly, with a shrill, crystal-like scream echoing through those rocky passes. The bandit chief had democratically offered to throw dice for the woman, but the bandits were not fools. They were well aware of Pepe's penchant for fair women.

So for a little more than five months she had been Pepe's woman. In her mind those months were murky and indistinct; even the memory of Pepe's whip had lost its edge. Not even a sense of shame had survived that long environment of restless motion; they were always on the move, from camp to camp, village to village. Pepe Groz and his men, and his horses, and his servants, and his woman. She did not grieve long for her murdered husband. Soon she did not remember him at all. A single persistent thought kept her

71

going. All things—even this—must end. She did not really believe it, but it was the only hope she had, and she clung to it.

And she had not really believed that she could escape Pepe's camp that night, but she had tried it anyway, because she had long since made up her mind to try, at least once, and she was now too numb and tired to form new decisions or reverse old ones. She had simply walked away from them. Pepe and his men had been hunkering about a fire, drunk on pulque and loudly laughing at the bandit leader's crude jokes. And she had simply, stupidly, walked away.

Perhaps they hadn't seen her, or possibly they had seen her but had not suspected that she would try to escape. After all, where was there to escape to? In these mountains, alone, she would surely lose her way and die. Probably it had not occurred to them that death might be preferable to some things. Certainly it had not occurred to Jessie Marchand. In the space of five months there had been innumerable chances to stand on principle and choose death. She had never done it. The will to live is not so easily smothered.

Jessie Marchand looked at Richter and asked, "Do you understand that?"

Richter nodded. "Yes." He'd had his chance in Glory to stand on principle and die, but it had not occurred to him to do it.

"Frank's father didn't understand it," she said.

Her eyes became vacant as she recalled that day.

The priest in Coyame was a kind but practical man. The sudden appearance of this woman had thrown his mission into confusion. He had given her what aid he could, but it was clear that he found the situation awkward—and the delicate state of international diplomacy at that moment did nothing to make it less awkward.

As for the girl, she only wanted to return to familiar things, to feel herself in familiar surroundings, and to see familiar faces. The priest, when she had revealed her wishes, was clearly relieved. He would talk immediately to the authorities, he assured her. He felt that the authorities would be only too willing to make as little of the matter as possible. Satisfying himself that she had no people of her own, excepting her husband's father, that good priest started the ponderous machinery of government, and before many days a message was received by Max Marchand on the other side of the Bravo.

In due time the elder Marchand appeared in Coyame and came directly to the mission. He was still dusty from his travels when the priest took him to the secluded mission garden where his daughter-in-law was waiting. They did not embrace; Max Marchand was not a demonstrative man. For a moment he looked steadily at his son's widow and then muttered something about her looking well and that the priest and sisters must have done a good job with her.

Max Marchand was not a big man, but to Jessie he seemed like some stern giant with dusty beard and glittering eyes. "Tell me," he said at last, "about my boy."

She groped for the words which would tell him what he wanted to hear. After a valiant defense, she said, in which Frank had killed several of the bandits, he had died with a bullet in his heart, instantly and without pain. Max Marchand did not believe a word of it. When he insisted, she told him the truth.

He stood in grim silence, his fists clinched, staring blindly at the mission walls. "I see," he said at last. And he looked at her with eyes gone cold. "I see."

At first she did not understand. She had forgotten for the moment that Max Marchand's rigid self-righteousness and unbending code of morality extended to every corner of his everyday life. The people of the world, in the eyes of Frank's father, were either good or bad, with very few of the former and no in-betweens at all.

Jessie Marchand recalled that, suddenly and without warning, she had laughed. Laughed hysterically and uncontrollably, as Max Marchand's face grew red with outrage. Quite suddenly she had glimpsed this meeting between herself and her father-in-law in its true ironic light.

In his fury, Max Marchand had spat a name at her.

Her laughter shot up in pitch and was shrill. What had been in that strait-laced mind of his, she could not imagine. But somehow, in that world of black or white that was Max Marchand's, any *good* woman would gladly have died rather than submit to the attentions of an animal like Pepe Groz. But she had not chosen to die. She was still alive, and that was the thing that damned her.

She smiled at Richter, wearily, and shrugged.

There was not much that Richter could say. In the blatantly sentimental period that followed the war there were a lot of men like Max Marchand. He said, "No matter what kind of notions he had, you was still his son's widow. That's not the kind of thing that he could just overlook."

"Oh, he was ready to take me back across the Bravo and give me some money to keep me going for a while."

"Why didn't you go?"

"I did," she said to Richter's dim surprise. "It was worse there than it is here."

That was all she said, and Richter didn't have to be told the rest. Once he had known a woman that had been captured by the Comanches while the frontier army was away in the war. After Appomattox the army brought her back to her family, but she would have been better off with the Indians. She didn't last long, back in the bosom of her family. Her husband crept off one day. Shame-faced relatives took the children. Women who had been her friends now turned suddenly blind when she appeared. And the men looked at her in that unmistakable way.

Richter sighed to himself. The girl sat in a kind of numb silence. It had not been a pleasant story, and Richter was not without compassion, but he did have troubles of his own. Better to say nothing, he decided, and let the matter die quietly.

Chapter Four

Around midday Richter ate some liver hash, drank some pulque and coffee and practiced walking back and forth between the dobe walls. His knees were still weak. The pain in his shoulder was a long-fingered hand that reached all the way to his groin. But, taking it altogether, it looked like he was going to be lucky. The wound looked clean. He seemed no more feverish than was to be expected.

He began to get restless; and he gave a great deal of sober thought to that cold-blooded pal of Gold Tooth's.

That afternoon Jessie Marchand returned to the shack with some bad news and a bottle of tequila. The news was that the police had been in town that morning asking about Richter. Juan Gomez, Gold Tooth's pal, had finally made himself heard.

"And Don Antonio's in town too," she said, "with some of his vaqueros."

"Sounds like a regular fiesta," Richter said dryly.

"That's not all. Remember the man Cabot, that Kopec told you about? He's in town too."

Richter looked at her. Maybe, after a year of waiting and doing nothing, it was finally time to return to Glory.

"Kopec can get you a horse tonight," she told him. "If you're in shape to ride."

"I'm in shape. Tell Kopec I'll pay him for the horse soon's I can."

"I don't think you'll have to pay. He's getting the horse from Don Antonio."

Richter's head was beginning to ache. Cabot, Juan Gomez, Don Antonio—the whole business was becoming far too complicated for his liking.

The girl went back to Kopec's and Richter stared thirstily at the tequila but did not touch it. The days of carousing and mooning at the wailing wall were over.

For the first time in a year he let himself think about Udall and Emily and Glory and all the rest of it. The years after the Civil War had been restless years for men like Richter. He had drifted in and out of a hundred places before he finally found that mountain-rimmed meadow of which Glory was now the center and the heart. Richter had known from the beginning that this was the place he was meant to be. He and some old wartime friends, Hagle, Matthews, and Tinkle, had raised a few head of cattle and had set them on the pastureland to multiply. But they had started with Mex cattle and they had been diseased. Soon they had nothing.

Hagle, Matthews, Tinkle, and Richter. One reversal did not defeat them. They knew all about reversals, having served with the Texas Volunteers in Virginia.

Hagle had laughed it off—three years of back-breaking work—as if it were nothing. Hagle told them it was all a blessing in disguise, if they would only see it. The enterprise had been doomed to failure because they had gone about it all wrong. Thinking that they could start a big brand cattle operation with a handful of diseased Mex cows. That had been their mistake. What they needed was first-class seed stock.

First-class seed stock. Hagle was the young one of the bunch, his optimism was ever green and eager. But the right kind of stock cost big money. And in those days good men were starving in Texas.

Matthews had little faith in the notion. All they had between them was their horses and rigs. Matthews was the hard-headed ex-sergeant of cavalry; he knew better than anyone that an attacking force must have twice the strength of a defending force. Attacking that valley without money or stock seemed like so much foolishness.

Tinkle was the quiet one, the thoughtful one, of that ragtag quartet. It had been Tinkle's notion to spend most of their original stake on a single patch of land in the basin. The land itself was rocky and sterile and worthless, but it controlled the only live water to be found between those mountainous walls.

"Boys," Tinkle had said after a period of deliberate thought, as always, "Hagle's right about the Mex cattle, that's sure. But we still control the water. And water controls grass. All we need is the right kind of stock."

Matthews had snorted derisively. "This ain't no patch of Texas brush where cows run wild and all you need is a hard head and a throwin' rope to get your herd together. Any cows that find a home in this basin has got to be bought and paid for, and drove in."

Tinkle did not deny it. "Well, then, that's what we'll have to do."

Richter did not know much about cattle at the time, but he had lived among miners and did know about grub stakes.

Tinkle had grinned a curiously boyish grin at Richter. "That's the way I see it. A stake, not just for grub, but for a seed herd and everything else it takes to keep a cow outfit going until we can start to show a profit."

Hagle thought it was a fine idea, but Matthews was not convinced. "Where do you reckon we'd find a man to give us money and keep us goin', out of the goodness of his heart?"

"Not out of the goodness of his heart," Richter said. "He would have to have a piece of the business. An interest in any future profit there might be in this basin."

"In the end it all comes up against the same

rock wall," Matthews insisted. "Where we goin' to find anybody to give us money just on the *chance* there might someday be a profit?"

"Bankers do it all the time," Tinkle said in his quiet way. "The ones with foresight get rich doin' it. That's the kind of man we'd have to go after."

Something else occurred to the bull-headed Matthews. "All right. Say it works. Say we find some banker fool enough to give us money. When we get the cattle in here and he sees how they fatten on this grass, and how they're sheltered by the mountains, and all the rest of it—what's to stop him from crowdin' us out and takin' ever'thing hisself?"

"We own the water," Tinkle said patiently. "The source of the water, anyhow. And we won't be fools enough to give that up."

In the end Tinkle had won. They had agreed that it was better to own a part of a profitable cattle business than to own a whole empty basin by themselves.

Finding a man to listen to them had not been easy; getting him to actually put money into their scheme had begun to look impossible. And then one day, as Richter was discouragedly saying goodbye to an El Paso banker, the banker was saying, "It might be that your cattle scheme is all you claim for it, but it's too chancy for the common-run banker. Have you talked to Udall about this?"

Richter had talked to every banker in El Paso. He had not come across anybody named Udall.

The financier shrugged, not completely at ease. "Henry Udall. He is stopping at the hotel, with his son and daughter." He looked sharply at Richter. "The name means nothing to you?"

"This is the first I've heard of it. But I'd like to hear more, if he's interested in cattle."

"Mr. Udall," the banker said with a certain wryness, "is interested in anything that might turn a profit. Mind you, I've got nothing against profit. But some men are willing to do more, go farther . . ."

The banker, in his own timid way, was trying to warn him against Udall. Richter thanked him and went to the trouble of questioning a few friends. Mr. Udall turned out to be a very interesting kind of man. He had made a sizable fortune running northern blockades during the war, but he wore no country's colors. In cow-country parlance, he didn't sound like the kind of man Richter would want to ride with. But beggars, according to another old saw, could not be choosers.

They met late that afternoon on the gallery of the El Paso Del Norte Hotel. Even if he hadn't had the clerk point him out, Richter would have known him immediately. He was of medium height, on the bony side. His yellowish skin looked dry and taut, as if it had been drawn wet over the skeletal framework and allowed to cure in the sun. His eyes looked feverish, and at first Richter guessed that he was just getting over a spell of swamp fever, but he soon learned that this certain feverishness was as natural to Udall as breathing. His dress was expensive and well cut, but it looked bizarre against the dirt and dobe background of the border town.

He wore ruffled linen, a swallowtail coat and a modified stovepipe hat—the kind of rig that Richter hadn't seen in twenty years. He also sported a heavy gold-headed walking stick, the kind that southern gallants had once carried as a matter of course, but in this day of the single-action Colt, was as obsolete as a matchlock. Just below the gold head Richter could see the almost invisible seam, the breakaway section of the stick which was actually a scabbard for about twenty inches of Solingin steel. A sword cane! In the hands of another man it would have been laughable. But not in Udall's. Henry Udall, as Richter was to learn, was many things, but "laughable" was not among them.

He was alone on the gallery when Richter approached him. Alone, and gazing out at the dusty streets with a hungry eye—though it was said that he had just returned from south of the Bravo where he had delivered several wagon loads of arms into the hands of Mexican rebels, which must have been a very profitable little excursion.

"Mr. Udall."

Henry Udall turned his hawkish face toward Richter and nodded. Richter sensed that here was a man who would not like to lightfoot along the edges of a proposition. "Me and some pals of mine," he said bluntly, "have got a scheme that would make us all rich men—maybe very rich—but it needs money to make it work."

Another man would have dismissed him at once as insane, but Henry Udall was not of the common cut. He looked at Richter and asked in a quiet, dry voice, "How many pals?"

Richter told him about Hagle and Matthews and Tinkle.

Udall's casual interest was clearly diminished. "Four ways to divide a profit, not counting a fifth party to finance you? It would need a *very* large profit, Mr. . . . ."

"Richter."

"Mr. Richter. A very large profit, indeed."

"Tinkle says maybe half a million dollars, and Tinkle's got a head for figures."

Udall did not actually stare, but he did blink once and glance at Richter. Then, without offering Richter one, he selected a slender brown cigar from a leather case, carefully cut the tip and lit it. Richter told him about the basin and about their plan for stocking it with the right kind of cattle.

Udall's feverish eyes took on a curious glitter as Richter talked. He made Richter go back and describe the basin several times. It seemed that he was as interested in the basin's isolation and the great walls of mountains as in the profitability of the scheme.

"When may I see this place?" he asked at last.

For the first time in many months Richter tasted hope. "You're interested in stakin' us?"

"That depends. When may I see it?"

It would hurt nothing to show the place to him. As Tinkle liked to point out, the basin was worthless without water, and the four of them owned equal shares of that. "I'll have to talk to my pards first, but I figger they'll go along. When you figger to start travelin'?"

"Tomorrow morning," Udall said. Then, with a barely civil nod, he said, "At first light, Mr. Richter. I'll meet you here in front of the hotel." He turned and strolled back into the lobby, that ridiculous sword cane tucked like a jockey's bat under his left arm.

The prospect of landing someone to finance them affected the various members of the partnership in predictable ways. Hagle was, as always, enthusiastic. Matthews was gloomily doubtful. Tinkle was pleased but was withholding final judgment.

85

It was Matthews who said, "I've heard about buzzards like Udall. In the war they played the North and South against each other and come up rich. He ain't the kind of bird I'd want to pard with."

"It ain't like we had a choice," Richter reminded him. "We've talked to most every banker in south Texas; most of them wouldn't even hear us out, must less lend us money."

"We could wait," Matthews said hard-headedly. "We could go to work and scrape up the cash ourselves, maybe."

Not likely, with trail drivers drawing from twelve to twenty dollars a month. Driving cattle was about all they were good for, now that there were no more wars to fight.

"We could wait," the ex-sergeant of cavalry insisted. "Sooner or later another banker'll come along—somebody we can trust."

But they couldn't believe that—not even Matthews. Time was the deadliest killer of all. The months and the years would come between them, destroying the only good thing to come out of a nightmarish war: that quiet, tough comradeship that only soldiers can know about.

The thoughtful Tinkle had said finally, "Anyhow, it can't do much damage to show the basin to Udall and listen to his proposition. If he's got one."

And Matthews knew that he had lost. All of

them had lost something, but they didn't know yet how much, or even what.

It was in the fiery light of an El Paso dawn, in front of the Del Norte, that Richter saw Emily Udall for the first time. She was fair, where her father and brother were dark. Her eyes were gray, her mouth suspiciously red. She wore a severe, high-necked traveling dress of black cord. A black pillbox hat sat straightaway on her tawny head. She carried a closed umbrella in the businesslike manner of a Prussian corporal with a saber.

She descended the Del Norte's steps on her father's arm and entered a high-wheeled carriage. She was not beautiful in the classical manner and did not try to be. But she managed her own kind of beauty which was totally unself-conscious and vaguely indolent. As she lounged back on the leather seat of the carriage she reminded Richter of a young female mountain cat warming herself in the morning sun. Here, Richter sensed, was a woman whose wish had never been thwarted, and who had every confidence that it never would be. In that raw, sun-blasted border town she looked as out of place as angel food on a private's mess plate.

Her brother Giles was cut of a darker, more austere cloth, from his father's pattern. Lean as a whip, he sat a blooded Morgan beside the carriage and watched the approach of Richter and his partners without so much as a nod.

Henry Udall said in a dryly accusing tone to Richter, "I said first light. You're late."

"We'll be later by the time you swap that rig for saddle animals. Maybe I didn't make it clear yesterday, but this basin of ours ain't exactly in the middle of things. There ain't no roads for carriages."

"Then roads will have to be built," Udall said tonelessly. "My daughter can't be expected to ride horseback, surely."

"I never expected we'd be carryin' a woman on this trip," Richter said, looking at Emily Udall.

She looked back at him for a moment, sizing him up, wondering idly if he might be worth a word or a smile. And finally she smiled, coolly, as impersonal as a drill sergeant. "Please don't worry yourself about me, Mr. Richter."

"I won't," he told her.

But that wasn't quite the case. Before their little foray was over he had put in quite a lot of worrying about Emily Udall.

An easy two-day trip from El Paso to the basin took slightly over four days, thanks to the Udall carriage.

Richter had anticipated trouble from his partners. These were tough men with minds of their own; their wills had been tempered in the fires of war. It was not likely, he had thought, that such men would willingly take orders from a war profiteer or his arrogant son or haughty daughter. He had been wrong.

He had forgotten what fools men could make of themselves because of women. But Udall was no fool. He conveyed his wishes through his daughter, and she expressed them as her own wishes, and they were attended to immediately. Richter was amazed, and faintly disturbed. A mile or so from the border town Emily Udall's aloofness toward the partners had moderated perceptibly. She could even manage a smile with some degree of warmth in it, if that was what the situation called for.

At the end of the first day she had Hagle and Tinkle leaping to her bidding like professional footmen. Even Matthews mellowed toward the Udalls. And Richter also. More than once he found himself jumping to attend to some whim of Emily's, only to realize later that Henry Udall was only voicing his own wishes through his daughter.

"Mr. Richter, up ahead seems like a lovely place to camp. Of course, it must be a long way from water, but . . ." One of them would gladly ride a tired horse another hour in order to fetch water for the night.

"You were right, Mr. Richter; we shouldn't have

89

brought the carriage. All this rocking and jolting; it's a wonder we haven't been thrown right to the ground. It would serve us right, of course." Like idiots, the partners rode ahead of the carriage, clearing the largest rocks from its path. Making the trip comfortable for Henry Udall.

Giles Udall remained something of a mystery to Richter. A great deal of his father's ruthlessness was etched in his thin face, but his true toughness was of a different order. It seemed to be in his blood, whereas Henry Udall's toughness appeared to be a matter of the mind. Giles' arrogance was that of royalty born to privilege. Henry Udall was the peasant who had fought his way to a kingship.

As they neared the battlements of those high Chanattes Henry Udall betrayed a kind of fixed excitement. As they made their way down the boulder-strewn slope, into the basin itself, those feverish eyes fairly glittered. He called to his son.

"Take the carriage," he said shortly. "I want the Morgan."

Giles knew better than to argue with his father. The elder Udall climbed down from the carriage and mounted the saddle animal. "You," he said to Richter, "come with me. I want to see this place of yours."

"It's a big place. Too big to see in one day."

"Then we'll take as long as necessary." He rode off, a lanky, scarecrow figure, but not a ridiculous one, confident that Richter would follow without question. As Richter did.

When they reached the floor of the basin they rested their horses for a while. Udall stared out at that vast, secure wilderness of brush and grass and gravel. "Where's the water?" he asked at last.

"Over there." Richter pointed toward the west wall of mountains. "It rises in a gravel bed, meanders east where you see the fringe of brush, and sinks again in another gravel bed."

"There's no chance that your rights to the water will be contested?"

Richter explained about state land. The land was for sale if you wanted to buy it, but all you needed was the little bit that controlled the water.

Udall wanted to see where the water originated, and Richter said, "It's farther than it looks."

"I don't care about distance. Show me."

They rode to that far western wall to the place where the water bubbled up cold and clear from an underground stream. Udall dismounted and tasted it and splashed his face with it and studied the glistening surface of the pool with a furious intensity.

They mounted and followed the shallow stream for almost an hour. Udall got down again and plucked some of the brittle grass. "You sure cattle can live on this?"

"They'll get fat on it, if they're healthy to start with. And if we don't overstock." Which hardly seemed likely in the foreseeable future.

"How much money do you need?"

Richter stared at him. "You made up your mind already?"

"Yes. How much?"

Richter swallowed with some difficulty. "We better ride back and talk to Tinkle. He's got it all figgered out."

That was the way it started. They should have known that nothing was ever that simple with a man like Udall. They should have realized right away that it was not Udall's kind of proposition. He was a war profiteer; his talent lay in recognizing opportunity when it appeared and seizing it by the throat. Bet his stack, rake in the money, and get out. A long-term return on a cash investment was foreign to his nature. They should have seen that. But they didn't.

For one thing, their existence as a partnership depended on Udall's backing. And the partnership was important, to all of them.

When Udall started something he saw it to the finish. He didn't stint. And he didn't waste time in indecision. Once he had seen the basin, all he wanted to know was how much.

Tinkle, the business mind of the partnership,

had done some fast calculating before Udall could change his mind. "Well," he said cautiously, "if we start with a thousand head . . ." Hoping for five hundred. Or even one hundred. "A thousand, say, at an average of seven dollars a head. You can get good stock for that, this close to the border . . ."

"How many head will this basin support?"

Tinkle shrugged. "Twelve, fifteen thousand, when it's built up."

"Why can't we start with five thousand?"

Five thousand times seven dollars a head, on top of other expenses! For a moment it seemed to take Tinkle's breath away. "We could start with that many, but a big risk would come with it. Even the old-time cowmen don't claim to know everything about cows. Sometimes they can surprise you, like that Mex herd surprised us. My advice is start slow, make sure we got the best kind of stock for this grass. And the best bulls. When we're sure we're on the right track we can stock heavier, addin' to the natural increase."

Tinkle's way was the plodding, careful way. Enterprise of such pale audacity that Richter wondered that Udall even listened. Instead, he nodded thoughtfully and said, "All right. Whatever you say."

That should have warned them. But it didn't. It was something like riding off a cut bank in the face of a blinding sun. Emily Udall had slightly dazzled all of them.

"About the water," Udall said. And in the back of his mind Richter thought, Here it comes. "In El Paso we'll get the necessary papers drawn up. We'll all be equal partners in the water rights, as in everything else."

Tinkle had smiled. Like Richter, he was mildly surprised that the subject hadn't been brought up before. He explained very carefully to Udall that what his money would buy was not a partnership but a percentage of the profits of the partnership.

Udall argued the point, but not for long, and not very hard. And another warning went unheeded.

They returned to El Paso in something less than two days. Udall, with his daughter's voice, did not complain so much about inconvenient campsites and the general discomfort of traveling in the wilderness. Richter and Tinkle selected the lawyers to draw up the binding agreements; they were not so bedazzled that they would turn that assignment over to a group of Udall sharpshooters. Udall offered only mild objections. Then he read the papers carefully and signed.

In a matter of hard cash, that flourish of the pen had cost him almost seven thousand dollars, on top of what it would cost to keep the operation going until they started showing a profit. The terms were much better than the partners had hoped for. They were slightly dazed at their sudden turn of fortune. Only the morose Matthews still held any suspicions in regard to Udall's good intentions.

Giles Udall went with them to that high, lonesome country below the Cap Rock where they bought their stock carefully, a head at a time, and paid premium prices without complaint. They were almost three months selecting and buying the herd and driving it back to the basin near the border.

Glory was more than half built by the time they returned with the cattle. Richter remembered very well the first time he saw it, and he recalled the stunned silence that had fallen around his partners and himself. Giles Udall looked at them with an amused half grin that almost always hovered about the corners of his thin mouth.

"Glory," Giles said. The five of them were sitting their horses on the crest of the north wall, staring down into that tawny, sun-drenched basin. There were two hired drovers in the drag and two more on the flanks holding the herd.

"Name of God!" Matthews exploded. "What is it?"

"A town," Giles said. "Or will be, when my father gets through with it. He wanted Emily to name it, and she called it Glory."

It didn't look like much of a town at the time. There were four frame shacks and a rawhide corral. The marvel was that there were buildings of any sort; the nearest timber was in the higher Chanatte peaks, and there were no sawmills there that Richter knew about.

"A town!" Hagle said with a wide grin. He was delighted.

Tinkle looked at Richter, and Richter turned to Giles. "There was nothin' in the agreement about buildin' a town."

Giles Udall shrugged. "That would depend on a judge's interpretation. According to the agreement, my father has the right to make improvements in the basin if it is necessary to protect his investment. Likely a court would decide that a town was such a necessity."

Richter didn't like it, and neither did Tinkle. Right from the beginning, Udall had started interpreting the agreement any way that happened to suit him. It was not the best way to start a business.

"Before you do anything foolish," Giles advised them, "wait. See what my father is doing and you'll understand that you'll all benefit from it."

In his own way Giles could be almost as

persuasive as his sister. The strength and brains of the family were Henry Udall's, but without the talents of his son and daughter he would not have been quite so formidable. The partners had waited.

Henry Udall had said to them, "The only way to do a thing is to get to it."

Well, that was basic enough. No argument there.

"I couldn't sit in El Paso holding my hands, while my son and partners were out working to bring the idea alive, could I?"

He insisted on thinking of them as partners. "This here's a cow outfit," Matthews had snarled. "We don't need a town here."

Udall smiled his cold smile. "That, sir, is where you're wrong. As you and your partners have noted, this basin is quite isolated and remote. Now it wouldn't be businesslike, would it, to travel all the way to El Paso every time a horse lost a shoe, or we needed a sack of cornmeal, or a posthole digger? We need the goods and services that only a town can provide." He gazed from face to face. "My name is not unknown in Washington City. We will have a post office here, as soon as some sort of town is established. And of course we must have roads—that won't be so simple, but it's far from impossible."

They stared at Udall in amazement. These things that he proposed were clearly impossible, but they knew that he would somehow accomplish them.

The hard-headed Matthews had growled for the second time, "We don't need a town. The cowhands can build their own shacks or dugouts to sleep in. We can throw up a shelter of some kind to keep the supplies in—what few supplies we need. As for a post office . . ." He laughed harshly. "None of us has got a letter from anybody since the war."

Udall sighed and shook his head. "Mr. Matthews, perhaps you and your partners are content to continue your slipshod business ways . . . which have already driven you into one bankruptcy. I am not." His tone was mild, but his eyes were like steel spikes. "I make it a practice," he said, "never to allow another's ignorance to jeopardize my investment. We will have our town here, and certain other improvements, also, or there will be no cattle operation in this basin."

Tinkle, in his quiet way, asked, "Isn't it a little late for that? We already have the cattle."

"Test me," Henry Udall said coldly.

Tinkle looked at Richter. There were, Richter knew, times when a man would destroy himself rather than give in. Apparently this was such a time for Udall. Richter didn't know why but this town was as important to Udall as the cattle operation—perhaps more so. If it was that important to him he could tie up the operation, in one court or another, until all the partners grew gray beards.

"We'll talk it over," Richter told him.

Udall relaxed and smiled his cold smile. He knew that he had won.

Chapter Five

A cold wind swept across the Bravo, and Richter huddled close to the small fire in the corner fireplace. Finally the girl returned with beer and tacos, but Richter wasn't hungry.

"What time is it?"

"It's almost dark." She didn't like the way he looked. The pale line around his mouth, the spots of color on his cheeks. "How do you feel?"

"Fine. Did Kopec get the horse?"

She nodded. "From Don Antonio's personal riding stock. A Thoroughbred, I think." She paused. "You sure you don't want something to eat?"

"I'm not hungry. What about the gunslinger—Cabot?"

"Kopec lost track of him. He doesn't seem to be in Prosperidad. On the other hand, nobody saw him leave."

A man like Cabot, if he wanted nobody to see him, then nobody saw him. "What about Gold Tooth's pal . . . what's his name?"

"Juan Gomez. He's down at Paco's getting drunk and bragging about how he's going to kill you. The police think you crossed back over the Bravo. At least that's what they told Kopec."

"Dark," Richter heard himself saying stupidly.

He hadn't realized that it was that late. With the roof about to fall on him, he had been sitting there all day doing nothing, thinking about Glory, and all the rest of it. Things better forgotten . . . if he could only forget.

"Don Antonio's ready to help," Jessie Marchand said. "He had the word passed along to Kopec."

Richter shrugged. If Don Antonio had ever owed him anything, the debt had been paid a hundred times over.

The girl folded her hands nervously. Then, from a clay jug, she poured some beer and drank it. "Do you aim to cross the Bravo?" she asked.

He grinned faintly. "Something I've been puttin' off for a year, almost. Now the time's come."

"You know what you'll be running into?"

"I can guess." He tried some of the beer, but it was stale and sour and didn't set well on top of the liver hash. He looked at the tacos but couldn't bring himself to try one.

"Kopec says this is a serious thing. He says if you cross the river you'll get yourself killed. He says it's dangerous enough, you hanging around on the border. But to cross the river . . ."

"Kopec," he said flatly, "is an old woman."

"Just the same, it stands to reason. Not knowing what they've got set for you, what chance have you got?"

He looked up, beginning to understand. His face grew hard. "That bohunk. One of these days I'll kill him."

"He's trying to help you."

"He's stickin' his big nose into what's none of his business. Kopec sent you to the hide and tallow dealer, didn't he?"

"It wasn't anything," she shrugged. "He was just pulling out for the other side."

"It'll be something when he gets back. Anything he does, he'll expect to be paid for."

She looked at him in a curious way and smiled very faintly. "Cantina girls soon learn to look out for themselves; so don't fret about the hide and tallow man." She made an impatient gesture, as though rubbing out something that she had written on a slate. "The thing is, he'll be coming back day after tomorrow. He crosses the river at Bonito. You know a place in Bonito called the Internacional?"

The Internacional was sort of a Mex wagon yard where mules and peons stayed. Richter knew where it was.

"Day after tomorrow," she said again. "After dark, you meet him there. He promised to keep his eyes and ears open. If there's anything doing on the other side he'll know about it."

Richter was furious that she had done this on his account. Even if it saved his life. She had no right to throw herself to a stinking hide and tallow dealer because of him.

She looked at him and read his mind. "I told you," she said wearily, "cantina girls learn to look out for themselves."

"Look," he said grimly, "is Don Antonio still in town? You think you can arrange for me to talk to him before I pull out tonight?"

She had read his mind again. "Richter, Richter," she said softly, as though addressing a child. "No wonder you're in hot water all the time. You're like a baby with its mother. You think people are good. And when you see the rottenness in them you're hurt."

Richter stared at her. There was something in what she said. Certainly he had let people fool him, and they had hurt him.

"Sure," she said, "you could probably talk Don Antonio into taking me with him to his ganaderia. But what then? You don't think he could hide what I am, do you? You don't think his family would accept me, do you? And the servants— they would despise me most of all."

Every word she said was truth, and Richter knew it. She was trapped, as he was trapped. Except that her entrapment was much more final than his. All he had against him was Udall and the governments of the United States and Mexico. She had the moralists.

Time dragged and Richter began to get jumpy.

The pain in his shoulder nagged at him and peeled his nerves. Perhaps an hour had passed since the girl had returned from the cantina.

"Where the hell is Kopec?"

"He'll be here when he thinks it's safe."

"It's dark, ain't it? That's as safe as it's goin' to get."

There was a rap at the door and both of them turned to stone. After a moment Jessie Marchand asked, "Who is it?"

A woman answered in rapid Spanish; it was one of Kopec's Mex cantina girls. Jessie Marchand motioned for Richter to stand back against the wall, then she went to the door and opened it enough to talk through. The Mex woman spoke a few sentences, slowly, so that the Marchand woman could understand, then she disappeared in the night.

Jessie Marchand bolted the door. "That was Marquita. The State Police are in town again. Kopec says to sit tight and he'll bring your horse when everything's clear."

The police again. It would be the final bitter irony, to wind up in front of a firing squad. How Udall would laugh over *that!*

"Maybe you better have a drink," the girl said.

Richter shook his head. For a year he had been drinking and crying over the fix he was in. He sensed that if he was ever to get himself straightened out he would have to do it sober.

He paced back and forth across the hut's dirt floor.

"Sit down," the girl said at last. "You're working yourself into a fever."

She was right. Richter could feel the dry heat in his face. But when he tried to sit and be quiet he found himself thinking again of Udall.

She said indifferently, "Sometimes it helps to talk."

"Talk about what?"

She shrugged. "Whatever's on your mind. The place called Glory, the man called Udall. Whatever it was you ran away from. Whatever it is you'll be running back to."

Looking at her coldly, snakelike, he fumbled for a harsh, black cigarrillo and lit it. "Talkin'," he said at last, "won't help."

"It beats running a fever."

Suddenly he grinned. There was an inner toughness, a soldier-like toughness, about her. He had never encountered it in a woman before, and he decided that he liked it. "You might have somethin'," he said. "But there's nothin' as fretful as listenin' to somebody cry hard times."

"I don't have anything better to do. I told Kopec I wouldn't be back to the cantina tonight."

He sat on the edge of the bed and gazed blankly at the dobe walls. Then, in a voice that was slightly cracked and pitched higher than common, he heard himself saying, "To begin with, you have to see her to understand how it happened."

That startled him. He hadn't realized until that moment that Emily Udall had been in his mind.

The partners had thought that Udall would soon weary of playing God in such a small world. It didn't occur to them that a man with Udall's wealth and power would actually move his family to that remote place and live there. They were wrong on both counts.

Big Studebaker freighters loaded with lumber and hardware and furnishings began rumbling down that perilous slope to the basin. Udall took only a superficial interest in the cattle. In the spring he was disappointed with Richter's calving report and ordered another thousand head of she-stuff and quality bulls brought down from the Panhandle. Army contractors from Fort Bliss heard of the operation and sent feelers out to Richter. But Udall wasn't interested in selling. At the moment he was interested only in buying and building. Profits, he said, would come later.

At the end of the first year the basin had undergone considerable change. There were six small rawhide buildings in Glory now, and that seemed to be just the way Udall wanted it. On one side of the street that Udall had personally laid out was a general merchandise store, a bath house-barber shop combination, and a harness and saddle shop. On the other side was combination saloon-eating house, a blacksmith, and a make-do wagon yard with some feed stalls and a shed and a rawhide corral. That was Glory, a town created out of the whim and the money of a single man.

The Udall house was the classic Texas shotgun ranch house, backed by a number of small sheds and corrals, situated on a piece of high ground overlooking the town. It was poorly built of rawhide lumber, and Udall made it clear that it was only a temporary arrangement, something to shelter his family until a fitting place could be built. Already he had imported a number of Mex workers to dig clay and shape dobe blocks and bake them in the sun.

Richter and Matthews and Tinkle did not see much of the town or the Udall residence. Most of the time they were out with the cattle, busying themselves with colicky cows and horn-fly grubs and half a hundred other miseries that cattle are heir to. Hagle, for some reason, had been singled out for duty at the Udall headquarters. The other partners had no special objection to this, as Udall had replaced Hagle with four first-class Mex vaqueros.

They watched over the cattle as if those contrary beasts were of their own blood. They established a kind of sub-headquarters far from Glory, almost against the east wall of mountains, and they systematically moved the cattle from one strictly defined place to another, assuring themselves that the quality of grass and water was the same in all parts of the basin.

One day Matthews rode into camp with the news that Udall had moved in several Mex families, allotting them parcels of land against the west wall. Farmers, Matthews said, spitting as he said the word, in the manner of a true cowman. What's more, Udall had set them to work digging irrigation ditches.

The three partners looked at one another meaningfully. If they meant to stock the basin to capacity it was not a bad idea to bring in a few landgrubbers to raise extra feed for the cattle. But they didn't like the idea of Udall—a non-partner, despite his financial backing—trenching water out of the main stream without so much as a word to any of them.

"Seems like there's some things," Richter said quietly, "that Mr. Udall has trouble gettin' through his head. Maybe one of us better ride into Glory and get him on the right track."

Richter was the one to go. Udall was his responsibility, since he was the one who convinced the others to accept his backing.

All six of Glory's business houses were in place by this time. There was even a watering trough in front of the general merchandise store. And the wagon yard owner had added two camp shacks to accommodate visitors. Richter shook his head in dumb wonder. He counted back in his mind and discovered that just eighteen months ago there had been nothing at all in this basin—except for the four partners and half a hundred dead cattle.

At this time Henry Udall was still a complete mystery to him. Why he had insisted on moving his family to this place, building a town where there were not enough people to support a single general store, Richter could not pretend to understand. He reined up at the end of the brush-grown street, gazed wishfully at the barber shop and bath house. After weeks in camp he smelt more cow than human, and he was aware of the griminess of his clothing. But he decided that a bath could wait. He reined toward the Udall house.

Higher on the slope where the original house was built he saw Mex laborers digging the foundations for a new, larger, and finer house of two-foot-thick adobe blocks.

It was a mild, still day in that sheltered basin. As he mounted the slope he saw Udall and an Army officer and Giles Udall lounging at a table in the shade of the dog-trot. There was a fourth man with them, a young civilian got up in the same expensive but archaic rig that was almost a uniform with the Udalls. This well-dressed, well-scrubbed, gleaming and highly polished young gentleman was Hagle, the youngest member of the partnership.

Richter tied up at the side of the house and headed toward the dog-trot. He couldn't imagine how Hagle had got himself so duded up. His young partner squirmed self-consciously as he approached and Richter grinned. *This,* he thought, will be somethin' to tell when I get back to camp. Tinkle and Matthews would never believe it!

The officer was a ruddy, gray-haired major of cavalry. Probably from Bliss, Richter thought. A long way from home. Giles Udall was Giles Udall, cool as always and secure in the knowledge that he was a Udall and that nothing could touch him. Henry Udall gazed with disapproval at Richter's grimy appearance but made an effort to be civil. He introduced Richter to the major, whose name was DeQuille, without explaining that Richter was one of the partners. Maybe, Richter thought with dim amusement, he didn't want to embarrass Hagle. The major was not very interested. Obviously he thought that Richter was one of Udall's hired hands.

Mex servants scurried back and forth from the cookhouse, loading the table with slivered ham, pork cracklings, salted pine nuts, and fried and salted tortillas, among several other dishes that Richter could not identify. They were sipping minted bourbon, and Richter gazed admiringly at the Tennessee label on the bottle, but no one asked him to join them.

Henry Udall rose from the table and excused himself. He strode directly to one of the corrals behind the house, and Richter followed, reluctantly, after another longing glance at the bottle.

"What is it?" Udall asked bluntly.

Suddenly Richter didn't want to come directly to the point. "What's that Major What's-his-name doin' here?"

"Major DeQuille is my guest," Udall said acidly.

"Is he buyin' stock for the Army?"

"Of course not," Udall said loftily. "The major's presence here is social." He seemed to take special pride in having an Army major in Glory for purely social reasons. At the time Richter accepted it as another of Udall's eccentricities with no special meaning.

"All right," Richter shrugged. "Maybe you can tell me how come Hagle's got hisself rigged out like a riverboat gambler, here in the middle of nowhere?"

"The point is," Udall said with some feeling, "that Glory is no longer the middle of nowhere. It is the middle of *some*where and it will become more so as time goes on . . ." He pulled up sharply. "But my social activities would not appear to be any of your concern. I am certain that you did not ride in from camp to ask idle questions."

"You're right," Richter said, with sudden bluntness of his own. "I just heard you're bringing in Mex families to farm the lower end of the basin. I wanted to make somethin' clear to you. This ain't your basin. And it ain't your water that you're trenchin' off to grow corn. Any time you take a notion to touch that water you'll first come to me and my pards and see what we say about it. Now have you got that clear, once and for all?"

It was fascinating to watch the blood drain from Udall's face. It had been a long, long time since anyone, anyone at all, had talked to him like that. His lips were compressed and almost blue.

There was the sound of laughter from beneath the dog-trot. Richter turned and saw that Emily Udall had joined the party. The men were standing and smiling widely. Richter seemed to see a hungry glint in the major's eyes.

"Just keep it in mind," Richter went on in the same blunt tone, "that you are not a member of this partnership. You are an outsider. We'll take your money, and we'll raise our cattle and in due time we'll make you a profit. But you're an outsider. We don't want you to forget it again."

Udall's white face went almost green with this final impertinence. "Mr. Richter!" he said quietly, faintly hissing. "Would it surprise you to know that I *am* a partner. At least, for all conceivable practical purposes I am."

Richter stared at him. "You're loco."

Udall smiled a razor-edged smile. "We had meant it to be a secret for a while, but perhaps you ought to know . . ."

A certain iciness entered Richter's bloodstream as he waited for Udall to go on. "My daughter," Udall said, "will soon be the bride of your friend, Mr. Hagle. Think about that, Richter. Does that suggest anything to you?"

With that question and a half smile on his thin lips, Udall returned to his guests.

For some time Richter was unable to think at all. He simply couldn't believe it. Hagle married to Emily Udall? Ridiculous! But in the back of his mind he sensed how thoroughly such an alliance could wreck the partnership. Udall, with one foot in the door, would somehow find the leverage to ransack the entire operation. Richter didn't know how he could be so sure of that. But he was sure.

Jessie Marchand was at the fireplace boiling coffee, her back to Richter. An uneasy silence was growing up around them. "Did they get married?" she asked, turning to look at him.

Richter was looking not at her but through her. He nodded absently. "Yes. They got married."

"Then what happened? That must have been three, four years ago." She smiled wanly. "It's a long honeymoon that goes three, four years. How's your friend Hagle like being Udall's son-in-law?"

"Hagle's dead."

It had been a long time since he had allowed himself to think about it just like that, bluntly, with no trimmings. As a matter of fact, it had been a long time since he had allowed himself to think about much of anything.

"I'm sorry," Jessie Marchand said quietly. From his tone she had guessed how close those original partners had been. Hagle, Matthews, Tinkle, and Richter.

Richter's thoughts went back in time to the day of the wedding.

It had been a big day for Glory. For almost a week private carriages had jolted over Udall's new road to the basin. Influential businessmen and Army officers jostled one another for looks at the coolly beautiful bride and the handsome young groom. All those who had received invitations were in attendance—a few men had already learned, to their grief, that it did not pay to ignore a Udall summons.

Matthews and Tinkle and Richter were guests, but not important ones. That night they joined the drinking and toasting long after the happy couple had departed for El Paso. There had been plenty of whiskey, good whiskey, but curiously, Richter could not get drunk. He located Tinkle and dragged him away from the house. Tinkle's face was slack, his eyes glazed. His brand new linen, bought especially for the occasion, was wilted and soiled.

"Let's get away from here," Richter told him.

Tinkle nodded dumbly. Richter saw that he was drunk, as were the statesmen and businessmen and officers beneath the many swinging Japanese lanterns near the dog-trot.

"Where's Matthews?" Richter asked.

Tinkle gazed toward the dancing lights and shook his head. They went back to the house and found Matthews flat on his back near the front gallery. The man who had survived countless murderous cavalry charges had been overcome by an endless flow of Tennessee whiskey. Months later this was something that crossed Richter's mind several times.

They soaked the ex-sergeant's head in a watering trough, then they got their horses and left the celebration. They returned to camp and built a fire and made coffee and pretended that everything was fine. Everything was not fine. A member of the main body had been removed. They could feel the kind of chilly ache where Hagle had been, the way a man might for several months feel the pain of an amputated foot. No one had said it yet, in so many words, but Hagle was gone. The partnership would never be the same again.

They hunkered in silence around their fire, burning their lips on scalding coffee. "I never figgered he'd go quite this far," Richter said. "Udall," he added when the others looked questions at him. "They're a cold-blooded family, all right, and I don't understand them any more than I did the first day I seen them."

Matthews came erect, his eyes slitted. "Cold-blooded, how?"

"Why do you think Emily Udall suddenly decided to marry Hagle? The water rights, that's why."

"That's a lie," Matthews said coldly. "A girl like Emily Udall wouldn't do a thing like that."

Richter was stunned. Matthews' outburst had sounded like the ugly rumble of his own world crumbling. "I didn't know you felt so strongly about it," he said.

"I don't feel any way at all," Matthews told him. "But from here on out, watch how you talk about ladies." The ex-sergeant lurched to his feet and stalked off into the night.

"What brought that on?" Richter asked in a stunned voice.

Tinkle smiled faintly. "You ain't been in camp much the last month or so. Emily Udall and her brother ride out this way sometimes. Giles usually corners me and talks about business, which he don't care a damn about. Emily usually gets Matthews to ride out with her and show her the basin—if you know what I mean."

If it had been anybody but Tinkle, Richter would have called him a liar. But Tinkle had a way of seeing people through amazingly clear eyes, and Tinkle, in those days, didn't lie. "She was playin' up to Matthews while aimin' to marry Hagle?"

Tinkle smiled his chilly smile. "I know how it sounds. Maybe it's a more cold-blooded family than you think."

Richter sat for some time, frankly worried. "What does it mean?" he asked.

Tinkle shrugged. "Udall wants this basin. And he'll do anything to get it."

"But *why?* Hagle's still the partner, not him."

"But if something happens to Hagle . . . ?"

Richter paled. "Exactly what're you shootin' at?"

"Ghosts and spooks and shadows mostly." Tinkle laughed, but the laughter had a hollow ring. "But it looks like Udall's out to bust up the partnership, and he don't care how he does it."

"Why should he go to such lengths? The cattle operation just ain't that important, especially to a man with Udall's money."

Tinkle sat for a long while looking into the fire. "I don't think it's more money he's after. It's name he wants now, and respect, and position.

All his life he's been undercuttin' old pals, stabbing friends in the back. He was a poor boy that started with nothin', a nobody. Now he's somebody, and he wants folks to know it. I guess that goes for Giles and Emily too."

Richter remembered the hungry look in Udall's eyes when he had first seen this basin. Here a man could be king, almost in the literal sense. A few poor Mex families to raise his feed, some vaqueros to tend the cattle, a few down-and-out storekeepers down in Glory—every living soul directly under the thumb of Henry Udall. Richter nodded slowly. Yes, he could see how such a situation could appeal to Udall, and maybe to Giles and Emily too.

"If something happened to Hagle," Tinkle said, returning to Richter's question. "I've got the ticklish feelin' that Udall's got his finger on half the lawyers in Texas and maybe some of the judges. If Hagle died, would his share of the water go to his widow or to his partners?" He laughed that hollow laugh again. "Shut your eyes a minute. Imagine a courtroom with twelve woman-hungry men in the jury box, and Emily Udall, all in black and very pale, there in front of them. Who do you figger they'd give Hagle's share to?"

Richter had no trouble getting the idea. "You think that's what the Udalls will try?" They looked at each other sharply. Here it was Hagle's wedding night and they already had him dead and buried and the surviving partners fighting the widow for the water rights. "I mean, even if Udall somehow got Hagle's share, he'd have only a quarter of the partnership. We could out vote him."

Tinkle looked at him for a long while. "We'll see," he said finally. ". . . we'll see."

For a while it seemed that nothing important had changed. Hagle still stayed close to headquarters while the other partners ranged the basin. Matthews had located a patch of loco weed at the north wall and he and Richter had carefully trenched around it and were burning it off in order to keep the poisonous weed from spreading. They were beating at the edges of the fire with wet towsacks when they saw Hagle riding toward them.

Matthews straightened up and wiped his sooty face. "Well," he said dryly, "if it ain't *Mister* Emily Udall, ridin' out to see how us workin' folks are doin'."

Richter had almost forgotten the way Matthews had acted on the night of the wedding. Since that time the ex-sergeant had kept a closed mouth about it, and Richter supposed that he wanted to let the matter drop.

It was clear now that Matthews had not forgotten anything at all. He was still sore at

Hagle because of the younger man's privileged position at Udall headquarters, but most of all he was sore at Hagle for marrying Emily Udall. All of them, even Richter, still thought of Hagle's wife as a Udall.

Hagle reined up beside the fire. A finger of uneasiness went up Richter's back when he saw the set look of the younger man's face. In all the years since the war not a word of anger had passed between the partners, but Richter sensed that that condition was about to end.

Hagle sat very erect in his silver-mounted saddle, staring directly at Matthews. Matthews returned the look and spat at the ground. "Well," he drawled, "I'm kinda surprised the Udalls give you leave to ride so far from headquarters all by yourself."

Hagle flushed but his voice was quiet and cold. "I came to see you, Matthews. It's the last time I'll be makin' the ride for this purpose. I came to tell you to stay away from my wife. I don't aim to warn you a second time."

"Warn" was an unfortunate choice of words on Hagle's part. It was just possible that an ex-sergeant of cavalry might listen to a suggestion, or a request, or a plea, but never to a warning. He laughed suddenly, derisively. Hagle, his face burning, looked as if Matthews had spit in his face.

Hagle spoke, sounding as if he were slowly

choking. "I mean it, Matthews. You bother my wife once more and I'll kill you." He wheeled his mount without another word, heading back for Glory.

Matthews stared in grim amusement. "Can you imagine that! A dudded up drummer boy threatenin' to *kill* me!"

"It wouldn't be the strangest thing that ever happened," Richter said. Then, very cautiously, he asked, "Matthews, is there anything goin' on between you and Mrs. Ud . . . Mrs. Hagle?"

Matthews had laughed, but the amusement had gone out of his eyes. "Richter," he said, "it really ain't none of your business, is it?"

"The partnership is my business."

"This ain't partnership, it's personal."

That was that. They went back to fighting the fire that they had started.

Later Richter learned from Tinkle that Emily and Matthews were still taking their rides together, just as they had done before she had become Mrs. Hagle.

Richter asked Tinkle, "Are you thinkin' what I'm thinkin'?"

"Exactly. If somebody wants to bust up the partnership, there ain't no better way to go about it."

"You think it would do any good to talk to Matthews?"

Tinkle shook his head. "Anything you say

121

against Emily you'll have to back up with gunplay. You know Matthews. First the Army was his life. Then the partnership. Until now a woman like Emily—or any kind of woman—had never looked at him. You can't blame him for being impressed."

"I can blame him for bothering another man's wife."

Tinkle had smiled his quiet smile. "I don't think," he said, "that's just the way it works." He sighed and spread his hands in front of him. "We're trapped, Richter. We're in this thing too deep to back out. Unless maybe you want to sell out to Udall—and I can see you don't. And neither do I. Just the same, Udall owns a piece of us now, and before long maybe he'll own a bigger piece."

"What do you mean by that?"

Tinkle said nothing. But a week later when they found Hagle and Matthews shot to death, Richter began to understand.

Chapter Six

Richter paced the floor and hugged his throbbing shoulder and smoked cigarrillos. Jessie Marchand was still at the fireplace, idly stirring the glowing coals. They were waiting for Kopec to send someone with the horse.

"Who killed them?" Jessie Marchand asked at last.

Richter glared angrily. "They shot each other, what did you think? Where is that lazy bohunk?"

The girl turned. "Shot each other?"

"Of course. That was the way it had to happen. Sooner or later they had to kill each other. That was the way Henry Udall had planned it."

"Or his daughter."

Richter was silent for several minutes. It was his opinion that Emily Udall was not capable of loving anyone but herself and her father and her brother. But he didn't want to talk about it.

"With just the two of you left," Jessie said, "where did that leave the partnership?"

After the deaths of Hagle and Matthews, Richter and Tinkle soon realized that Udall wasn't out to merely break up the partnership, he was out to destroy it. The question of the moment was how Emily and the remaining partners would divide up the water interest. None of the original partnership had any heirs, so there was at least a very good chance that a court now would cut Matthews' part three ways. Udall's portion was getting bigger, but not nearly big enough. He would need at least fifty-one percent of the water rights to know without a doubt that the basin was finally his.

First he tried to buy Richter's interest, and then Tinkle's, without luck. It was several weeks after the deaths of Hagle and Matthews that Richter and Tinkle met at their camp for a talk. It was the last serious talk they had.

"They're goin' to beat us, Richter," Tinkle said in almost a casual way. "They know what they want and they want it bad. We're standin' in their way—one of us, at least. Sooner or later they'll find a way to turn us against each other, the way they did Hagle and Matthews."

"They won't turn us against each other," Richter had said with conviction.

Tinkle smiled. "I hope you're right. If you are, they'll have to kill one of us to get control. That might be where they'll make their mistake."

"They're too smart to try killin'. If one of us comes up drygulched, all the signs would point to them. That wouldn't help them any in gettin' what they want."

Tinkle was strangely quiet. Then he said, "I was up to the big house yesterday." That was what they called the new Udall place. "One of the Mex hands found me and said something was wrong at the big house and they needed me. But when I got there I saw that nothin' was wrong; it was just Emily Udall wantin' to talk."

Hagle had passed through Emily's life leaving hardly a trace. Even his name had been dropped. Richter said, "Talk about what?"

Tinkle seemed strangely self-conscious. "Nothin' in particular. But after a while I got the notion that bein' a widow was a lonesome business. I'll tell you somethin', Richter. Leadin' the kind of life we lead is a lonesome business, too."

Richter didn't have to have it spelled out for him. He had felt it too, the lonesomeness of a single man in an empty place. He had tried not to think about it—thinking about it was the thing that had killed Hagle and Matthews. Now Tinkle was telling him in a sidelong way that he was thinking about it too.

There was a curiously sad expression on Tinkle's long face. "I'll tell you somethin' else," he said at last. "If Emily Udall ever asks me for my share of the partnership I ain't right sure I wouldn't give it to her."

Once the same thought had crossed Richter's mind. But not any more. He was older than Tinkle; perhaps the loss of two comrades meant more to him. Richter grinned and felt as if his face were cracking. "Much obliged for tellin' me. But I don't know what to do about it."

"Neither do I," Tinkle said. They stared into the fire as though they were watching the world end.

It was perhaps a month after his talk with Tinkle that one of Udall's Mex vaqueros brought Richter the message. He was wanted at the big house on an urgent matter. Maybe the same kind of urgency that had drawn Tinkle there, Richter thought. Well, he might as well get it settled, once and for all.

But he didn't see Emily Udall at all. The vaquero took him to the general store in Glory. There was a curious gathering on the loading ramp in front of the store. There were several Mex hands, both vaqueros and farmers, and Udall himself and his son, and a bland, sleepy-looking man whose name turned out to be Venture. He was, as Richter soon learned, a deputy United States Marshal.

Deputy Marshal Venture gave Richter a slow, heavy-lidded stare and asked softly, "Your name, mister?"

Puzzled, Richter gazed about him at the curiously blank faces. "Richter," he said.

"Full name," Venture yawned.

"William Stuart Richter."

Venture belched comfortably and reached for a paper in his vest pocket. "Well, Mr. William Stuart Richter, I got here a warrant for your arrest. Now no trouble. No foolishness. And there won't nobody get hurt."

Richter was stunned. Some of Udall's vaqueros were nervously cupping the butts of their revolvers. "What am I accused of?" Richter asked in a voice that he hardly recognized.

"Ever'thing in its time, Mr. Richter." Marshal Venture scratched himself and smiled. "Now unbuckle your gunbelt and hold out your hands."

He no longer had a choice. The vaqueros had drawn their revolvers. Henry Udall and his son stood a little to one side of the gathering, smiling faintly. When Richter was disarmed and handcuffed he made himself look at the Udalls and ask harshly, "What the hell's this about?"

"No use takin' that tone," Marshal Venture said. "We got you dead to rights. Witnesses on both sides of the Bravo. We even found some of the money."

"What're you talkin' about!" Richter realized that he was yelling, but he didn't care about that.

"Don't reckon I have to tell *you*," the marshal said. "But I don't mind. Just so you know you can't pull no monkeyshines. I told you, we got witnesses. And we found some of the money in your saddle pocket."

Richter turned and saw a grinning vaquero holding up a leather pouch. He handed it up to the marshal and the marshal opened it. "I'll count it later," Venture said disinterestedly, "but I'd say offhand it's close to a thousand dollars, gold."

Richter had the frightening feeling that he was rapidly losing his mind. He wheeled on the Udalls and yelled, "What're you up to! What's goin' on here!"

The Udalls smiled securely and said nothing. Marshal Venture asked with maddening blandness, "Do you deny sellin' the cows and killin' José Brandes?"

"I never even heard of José Brandes! What cows!"

Venture clucked his tongue in disappointment. "Well, you can tell your story in court, but it won't do any good. You'll hang, mister."

In a red haze of rage, Richter made a break for it. The vaqueros excitedly clubbed him down and would have killed him if Venture had not stepped in.

When Richter regained consciousness he was handcuffed and lashed to a saddle. They were just easing their way down the outside wall of the basin. The marshal was taking him to El Paso to stand trial.

But that was not to be Marshal Venture's lucky day. About five miles from the basin rim an unseen rifle spoke flatly but with great authority, and the marshal pitched forward in his saddle, a bright crimson stain spreading between his shoulders.

Richter, still dazed from the beating, stared at

the rifleman riding toward them from a thicket of mesquite. The rifleman was the quiet, soft-spoken, harmless Tinkle.

Richter sat on the edge of the bunk and nursed his shoulder and listened to the humming silence that was Prosperidad at night. For almost an hour he had been talking. Talking to forget the pain in his shoulder. Talking to keep from exploding while waiting for Kopec to bring the horse. He felt faintly sick and his mouth was cottony.

Jessie Marchand had taken one of the hut's two chairs and was watching him carefully. "So your friend saved you from a hanging," she said at last.

Richter looked at her and suddenly laughed. It had a wild sound and he didn't like it. "My *friend*," he said wryly. "Good old Tinkle." Strange, in a way, that he had never learned to hate Tinkle. Even when he realized that murdering the marshal was all part of a plan—Tinkle's plan. The other part—the drummed-up charge of murder and theft was typically Udall. But killing the marshal had been Tinkle's own personal contribution.

Richter could still recall how stunned he had been, watching that deputy marshal dump slowly out of his saddle, dead even before he hit the ground. "God-a-mighty," he had said to Tinkle, "did you have to kill him!"

"He was takin' you to hang," Tinkle said.

"It was all a scheme of Udall's. A drummed-up charge."

"With Udall men on your jury, you figger that would of made any difference?"

No. Tinkle was right. They would have hanged him. One way or another Udall would have seen to it.

Tinkle had removed the handcuffs and cut him free of the saddle. "You can make it across the Bravo all right," he had said. "Keep goin' south and there won't be any trouble." Only later, when Richter's thoughts were better organized, did he realize how neatly he had been exiled.

"Was there actually a murder," Jessie Marchand asked. "Besides the marshal, I mean?"

"There was a murder, all right. One of Udall's vaqueros that didn't like the way things were going—his pards killed him, then swore it was me. Like they swore that I had been stealing cattle from the partnership and sellin' them across the Bravo."

The girl hesitated, then said, "Your friend, Tinkle. He killed the marshal and then made it look as if you had done it; is that what happened?"

"That's what happened. You're seein' through Tinkle a lot quicker than I did—but of course you didn't go through a war with him."

"But why did he do it? The girl? Emily?"

Richter laughed that chilling laugh again.

"I mean," she said, "the Udalls had arranged to have you hung. Why didn't he let it go at that?"

Suddenly Richter felt very old. "It wasn't like Tinkle. Murderin' a friend. Or standin' by and watchin' the Udalls do it. I give him that much—and it's little enough. In the showdown he did save me from a hangin'."

"And tarred you with a second murder."

Richter grunted. Tinkle was the last living man to remind him of the old life, the partnership. Maybe that was why Richter didn't want to hate him. There had been a comradeship there once, forged in war and tempered in reconstruction, a friendship so fast and tough that they had thought it was indestructible.

The girl was reading his thoughts again. "It's crazy, going back to that place again. With two murders and a rustling charge hanging over you."

It was crazy staying here on the border for a year, too, but he had done it.

She said, "You'll never get the basin back. I've known men like Udall; you can't beat them."

"You can kill them," Richter said. And that was what it boiled down to. The basin, the cattle operation—they no longer mattered. That had been a rosy vision shared by the four partners, and the partnership was destroyed. Killing the Udalls was as far as his thinking could go. It was

131

the only answer; it had taken him a year of exile to admit it.

"Richter," she said gently, "you'll just burn yourself out. You'll get yourself killed, and for nothing. Udall will still own the basin. Why don't you forget it and head down to Durango, or maybe Nuevo Leon, where they can't find you?"

His mouth curled in a completely humorless grin. "I've thought about it. It won't do. You can't cure a fever by tellin' yourself it's not there."

A nervous hand rapped lightly on the door. The cantina girl from Kopec's whispered, "Señor Richter!"

Jessie Marchand cracked the door and they talked for a moment in Spanish. Then she closed the door and said, "Kopec thinks it's all right. The police left an hour ago. If Cabot's in town, he's keeping out of sight."

"The horse?"

"Tied up behind the cantina, saddled and ready to go. Leave your own rig here."

With the girl's help Richter buckled on his .45. With considerable effort they got him into his tattered brush jacket. He took up his rifle and Jessie Marchand said, "Don't forget the Internacional in Bonito. If the hide and tallow dealer hears anything about Glory or the Udalls, he'll tell you."

"All right." He nodded impatiently and reached for the door.

"Richter . . ." He hesitated, and she said self-consciously, "Nothing, I guess. Watch out for yourself."

"Sure. I'll be seein' you." He managed a thin smile. The last place on Earth he wanted to see again was Prosperidad.

The horse was just where the girl had said it would be. It was a handsome chestnut, a Thoroughbred with a warrior's chest and delicate legs. The saddle was a heavy Mex affair, with a big balloon pommel, and bull-nosed tapaderos on the stirrups; the leather was beautifully tooled and mounted with silver.

Richter sighed. Don Antonio had given him the most cherished animal in his personal string, and a sizable fortune in saddlery. Richter would have much preferred a brush scarred cow pony with a forty-pound working saddle. But that was Don Antonio. Nothing but the best, where Richter was concerned.

Kopec was waiting at the back door of the cantina. He lit a black Mex stogie and studied Richter in the flaring light. "You sure you can ride?"

"I can make it to Glory. That's as far as I aim to go."

Kopec blew out the match and sighed. "If you

know a doc you can trust, you better look him up," Kopec said. "Anything else you need?"

Richter shook his head. "Just a boost to the saddle."

With Kopec's help he mounted awkwardly to the high cantled saddle. "I feel like a damn fool with a rig like this. Tell Don Antonio I'm obliged." The glowing tip of the stogie bobbed up and down as Kopec nodded. "So long, Kopec. I'll settle up with you some day, if I can."

"*Hasta luego*," Kopec said. He stood watching Richter ride down the west slope from Prosperidad, and when he could no longer see the rider or the chestnut he went back into his cantina.

Bonito was not Mexico and it was not the States. It was a border town, a breed apart. It held no disappointments or surprises for Richter; the Internacional was just the kind of mud-walled sty that he had expected.

And Pablo Murillo was one nervous and frightened, as well as evil smelling, hide and tallow dealer. "I tell you straight, señor," he hissed between decaying teeth, "I wish I never hear your name. I wish I never talk to that woman in Prosperidad!" He crossed himself superstitiously, an automatic gesture that had nothing to do with religion.

"Never mind that," Richter said, standing

carefully to windward. "What did you find out about Glory and the Udalls?"

What Murillo had found out was little enough, and that was far from comforting. He had gone right into the basin, hoping to do some business. There had been no business there for hide and tallow men. The cattle there were fat and healthy, and the owners were prosperous. Very prosperous.

Owners? Richter asked if Tinkle was the husband of Udall's daughter. Murillo grinned and rolled his eyes meaningfully. They were not married. The Udall woman—much woman! And the man, Tinkle. Murillo panted loudly, lolling his tongue. He laughed at his little joke. Murillo did not have to put his filth into words in order to be understood. Then, quite suddenly, he was frightened again.

In Glory, he said, to speak Richter's name was to spit filth. He had received some harsh treatment at the hand of Udall's vaqueros, merely because he had happened to mention Richter. They had questioned him sharply about Richter's whereabouts but were finally convinced that he knew nothing. They had let him go, but the experience had left him shaken. Now, he told Richter, go away and leave him alone. He wanted nothing more to do with this affair.

Did he know anything about a gunslinger named Cabot? Richter asked.

Murillo did not know Cabot. But he advised Richter, with feeling, to leave Bonito at once and take himself far away from Glory. He ducked his head, refusing to look Richter in the eye. He crossed himself again, quickly, as the Indians did when speaking of the dead.

So Tinkle was still alive and a part of the operation: Richter was not surprised. Tinkle and Udall knew too much about each other for one to trust the other out of his sight. The fact that Richter was just across the river, haunting them, must be a constant source of uneasiness to them. Richter wondered grimly how many times Tinkle had cursed himself for interfering with a process that would surely have led to Richter's death. For he must realize now, as Udall did, that Richter would have to die before any of them could have any peace.

Pablo Murillo was sidling away from Richter as though he were a known typhoid carrier. Richter looked at him hard and said, "This could be a very bad business. Very unhealthy for anybody that gets hisself caught in the crossfire, like they say."

The hide and tallow man blinked nervously. "No understand."

"The girl in Prosperidad that put you up to this." Richter smiled thinly and drew a finger across his throat. "Very dangerous proposition."

Murillo stared. "Dangerous?"

"Look," Richter said confidentially, with as much warmth as he could muster. "You done me a favor, so I'll do one for you. Unless you're bulletproof, stay away from that cantina girl."

Murillo was worried but not as worried as Richter had hoped. It was too far-fetched, trying to link Jessie Marchand to Udall. Murillo would think about it for a little while and then forget it. He shook his head dully. "No, not dangerous. Not in Prosperidad."

Richter decided to be honest. He spoke quietly and with feeling. "Pablo, do you know what I'm wanted for, across the Bravo? On this side too, for that matter."

Pablo knew well enough that Richter was wanted for murder on both sides of the river. Richter watched his blank face become puzzled, and then worried, and finally frightened. Richter drew his .45 and casually rested the muzzle against Murillo's temple. "Pablo," he asked, "is there any doubt in that dirty mind of yours that I wouldn't kill you, if I took a notion?"

Pablo stared in terror. Richter moved the muzzle down along his cheek and let him smell the gun oil and steel. "If you go near that girl in Prosperidad I'll kill you, Pablo. I'll make a special point of it. I'll even break off my business with the Udalls. I'll hunt you, and I'll find you, and I'll kill you. That's all there is to it. You savvy?"

Murillo was sweating freely. He didn't understand all the fuss about a common cantina girl, but he understood the tone of Richter's voice, and the glint in his eyes. And he believed him. Lucky for Pablo. For Richter had meant every word.

"You understand me?" Richter asked.

Murillo nodded dumbly but quickly.

"All right, that's all. You can go."

Pablo needed no second invitation. He scurried like a grave rat, disappearing in the litter and dirt and misery that was the Internacional.

There was a rock crossing below Bonito that smugglers and rustlers and gun runners used from time to time when the border patrol was busy somewhere else. Richter watched the place from a distance. He saw two Mex vaqueros cross there, heading north. A peddler of some kind crossed in a dilapidated wagon, heading south. Around sundown two peons, or maybe bandits, appeared on foot driving a dozen scrawny steers. They crossed the river as if it had been an open highway and soon disappeared from sight.

An hour later Richter crossed. He was in Texas again.

The instant he touched the north bank he knew that he would not be leaving it again. Officially, he was a double murderer and a thief who stole from his own partners, and any man he chanced to meet was potentially a deadly enemy. Still, he knew that this was where he would stay—for as long as he lived.

The air in a man's homeland was sweeter than that of other places. And he was home again. No more wailing walls. No more of Kopec's rotgut tequila. He was home again. And this is where he meant to stay.

He felt better now, freer, though he knew that his dangers had multiplied on every side. Here there were no Don Antonios to watch over him. No Kopecs. And, for that matter, no Jessie Marchands.

He urged the chestnut up a rocky slope and put the river behind him as quickly as possible. Ahead of him lay broken country, scrub brush and boulders and miles of prickly pear. Farther ahead he could see the austere, purple range of the Chanattes. Beyond that was the basin and Glory.

He made dry camp that night and chewed some jerky and drank a little tequila that Kopec had thought to put in his saddle pocket. He watched the Chanattes go from purple to gaudy yellow as the sun slowly died. Then the mountains changed to somber gray, and finally black. And when the full weight of night was on that borderland a white moon appeared and touched those ridges here and there with silver. How many times he had seen them like that, from the wailing wall! Seen them and thought darkly of the day of his return.

Well, now he was returning.

He awoke the next morning with a heat-seeking lizard squirming beneath his injured shoulder. He felt like hell, his stomach sour, his face hot, his mouth dry. His shoulder didn't look so good, and it felt worse.

The chestnut was cropping bunch grass on the slope where Richter had staked it out for the night. He sat up slowly, thinking that the first thing he had to do was find some water for the horse and himself. Maybe he would feel better, with some hot coffee in his belly.

Cautiously, he started shoving himself to his feet. A thin, cold voice said, "Stay. Do not move."

Richter recognized the voice immediately. It belonged to the cool one, the one called Juan Gomez, the dead Gold Tooth's snake-eyed pard. Richter did as he was told. He sat very still.

He felt something small and round and cold bore into the back of his neck, and nobody had to tell him that it was the muzzle of a .45. Somewhere inside of Richter there was a silent rage clawing to get out. He controlled it with an effort. If Richter had his man pegged, Gomez would want to draw it out a little before killing him. Just the same, it was not easy to sit there on the ground trying to appear calm and unruffled, knowing that this nobody of a fourth-class bandit would very likely shatter all the fine plans that he had for the Udalls. And Tinkle. His old friend and wartime comrade, Tinkle.

Richter was surprised to hear his own voice, steady and unshaken, saying, "Just as a case of curiosity, boy. Was trackin' me down your own notion, or are you doin' a job of work for Udall?"

Gomez circled around to face Richter, but the muzzle of his .45 never lost contact with Richter's body. He squatted down directly in front of Richter, his face only inches away, the muzzle of his revolver pressing into the soft hollow of Richter's throat. He was grinning. This was something that he had been doing a lot of thinking about, and he meant to enjoy it.

"Udall," Richter said again. Speaking was difficult, with that muzzle pressing in between his breastbone and Adam's apple. "Are you one of Udall's boys?"

Gomez continued to grin but his eyes were blank. "You understand what I'm sayin'?" Richter asked. "You savvy American?"

Without losing his grin Gomez gathered his spittle and spat in Richter's face. Richter didn't dare raise a hand to wipe his face. He knew that Gomez knew what he was saying; he just wasn't interested. He only wanted to watch Richter squirm for a while on the hook, and then he would kill him. That would settle the score for Gold Tooth.

A sense of futility settled on Richter's shoulders like a heavy cloak. The thought of being killed by this sneering, grinning, low-grade badman was almost too much to bear in silence.

They studied each other for a moment. Gomez was quite young; not much more than a boy. Some boy, Richter thought grimly. He saw the greed in the youth's eyes. Right now Juan Gomez was thinking more about that handsome Thoroughbred and expensive saddle than he was about his dead pal.

"All right," Richter said, as if the whole thing was a matter of great indifference to him. "You got the drop on me, boy. I don't never argue with a loaded gun, especially when it's pointed dead level at my gizzard. You want money? I can get you money."

Greed and caution clashed in the youth's eyes—greed was the uneasy winner. "Tell me."

"For one thing I'm a big pal of Don Antonio's. You must of heard that much about me, back in Prosperidad. How about me writin' out a note for you to take to . . ."

Juan Gomez lost interest immediately. He grinned. He would settle for the expensive horse and the silver-mounted saddle and Richter's life.

Richter could feel the fight going out of him. He found it difficult to care what Gomez would do. His shoulder seemed to shimmer with pain, and that mattered more than anything, even staying alive. He looked at Gomez, and then, with an indifferent gesture, brushed aside the barrel of the .45.

The youth's eyes blazed. He was startled and angered; he had expected to see Richter whimper and beg for his life, but it was almost as though this giant gringo was *asking* to die. All right! Richter could see Gomez making his decision. If he wanted to die, Juan Gomez was just the boy to see to his wishes.

Richter gazed bleakly past the youth's shoulder, looking at the range of Chanattes and realizing finally that Udall was going to have his way. Then, from the side of his vision, another figure interrupted his study of those dark mountains. A tall, raw-boned man, looking faintly ridiculous in his narrow brim brush hat and his pony hide vest, came quietly up the slope.

There was nothing ridiculous in that long, horselike face and slitted eyes as he approached on Juan's rear. He looked directly at Richter, and Richter understood why the local peons had credited him with the evil eye. His eyes—blue, Richter supposed—were quite pale, and his face was cured by years of merciless sun to the color of old leather. The effect of such a combination was bizarre, like two pale lights peering at you from an approaching darkness.

Juan Gomez did not miss Richter's look of fascination. The youth grinned, thinking that it was a trick to divert his attention. Well, he would not be fooled. His finger tightened on the trigger.

The man in the brush hat and pony vest spoke quietly, in Spanish, when he was perhaps twenty yards from them. His .45 rested at peace in his holster, but a businesslike Winchester saddle rifle was in his hands. A professional never used a revolver if he could help it. And this man was a professional; it showed in the way he looked and the way he moved. And his name, Richter knew, would be Cabot.

Juan Gomez grunted, startled at the sound of this voice at his back. Cabot spoke again, sharply this time. The boy went rigid. Richter could see his mind whirling behind his dark eyes. He had prepared himself for the enjoyment of killing Richter the way another man might have prepared himself for a fine meal. He almost pulled that trigger, in spite of Cabot's command.

But at the last minute his finger froze. Cabot came a little closer and spit out a string of Mex words that went completely over Richter's head. But they had their effect on Gomez. With great reluctance, the boy holstered his revolver, his eyes flashing death and violence.

At last Juan stood, turned and looked at his new enemy. Cabot smiled frigidly. "Get out of my sight," he said in English, "before I do the Mex police a favor and kill you right here."

Gomez began backing away. He was a study

in hate and frustration, but he was not a fool. He knew doom when he saw it, and he saw it now in those pale eyes.

Richter sat hugging his shoulder without saying a word. He had found the by-play mildly interesting while it lasted but of no real importance. When the shooting was over, what difference would it make who had killed him? Gold Tooth's pal, or Udall's hired assassin.

Juan Gomez disappeared around the waist of the slope, and after a few minutes they heard the pound of hoofs heading south.

Cabot now turned his icy smile on Richter. "On your feet."

Richter looked at him. "What's the difference? You can kill me as easy one way as another. It won't make any difference to Udall."

Cabot seemed to study Richter's words, digesting them one by one. Finally his smile became a little less icy and a little more crooked. "You figger I work for Udall, is that it?"

"You ain't the first one."

In a coldly distant way this seemed to afford Cabot some faint amusement. "I see." He took something from his vest pocket and held it for Richter to see. It was the badge of a Texas Ranger. "I've been a long time gettin' my hands on you, Richter."

Richter stared at the badge for several seconds. It wasn't possible that the assassin with the evil eye could be a Ranger. But there was the proof in Cabot's hand. "Kind of poachin' on Mex property, wasn't you?" he said at last. "You must of wanted me pretty bad."

"Bad enough." Cabot started to pocket the badge, then changed his mind and pinned it on his vest.

Richter got slowly to his feet. "Well . . ." He managed a weary grin. "Thanks anyhow for not lettin' the Mex kid put a bullet in my gizzard. I guess you know about Gold Tooth."

The marshal looked blank, and Richter added, "Pablo Somebody. I shot him down at the horse tradin' corral at Prosperidad, and picked up a bad shoulder doin' it."

"That's somethin' for the Mex police to stew about." He took Richter's .45 and unloaded his rifle. Then he shouldered the heavy riding gear and started toward the horses. Richter followed. At the moment he was in no way to do much fighting or running.

There was kind of a tough, undefeatable irony here that Richter amused himself with for a while. He stood to one side, half-grinning as Cabot saddled the Thoroughbred.

"For myself," the Ranger said dryly, "I never could see the comical side of gettin' hung. But it takes all kinds, they say."

"I was just wonderin' why Udall bothers to hire men of his own, when the law does all his work for him. Even when it has to cross into another country."

"You'll remember it was north of the river that I arrested you, not in Mexico."

Richter shrugged with his good shoulder. Cabot gave him a boost to the saddle. Then the marshal got his own animal and mounted. "How do you feel?" he asked, gazing narrowly at the dirty paleness of Richter's face.

"All right. I'll live till the hangin', anyhow."

"I hope so," Cabot said.

Richter looked at him closely and for the first time saw the hate in those pale eyes.

Richter felt himself sinking in futility, like a drowning man going down in a warm ocean. Not until midday did it occur to him to ask, "Why'd you take a chance like that? Crossin' the river, I mean."

Looking straight ahead, Cabot said, "Venture was a friend of mine."

The name meant nothing to Richter. Somewhere in that year of exile the dead marshal's name had passed completely from his memory. Cabot glanced at him and saw that Richter had not understood, and the hate in his eyes focused down to needle points. "Sometimes I forget there are men like you, Richter. You pick your man, you murder him, shoot him in the back, and a year later you can't even remember his name."

The sleepy marshal that Tinkle had killed. Now the name came to him—but it was much too late to turn the point of Cabot's personal vendetta.

Toward the middle of the afternoon Richter became dizzy and all but pitched from the saddle. They stopped by a little gyp-water stream and boiled coffee and Cabot looked at the shoulder. He didn't look disturbed at what he saw, so Richter guessed that his most immediate danger was still ropes, not knives. "I forgot to ask," he said. "Where are you takin' me?"

"El Paso, to begin with."

"And then?"

"That depends on where they want to hold the hangin'."

That was the way it went the rest of the day. By nightfall Richter was too tired to care about anything but the pain in his shoulder. He got Kopec's gift of tequila from his saddle pocket and pulled on the bottle. Cabot made a fire, fried some fat Mexican bacon and boiled more coffee. Richter said at last, "I don't reckon you'd be very interested to hear that it wasn't me that killed your pal."

Cabot looked up from his cooking. "Not very."

"Now there's some things I *did* do. Like Gold Tooth, back there in Prosperidad. I killed him right enough. And one of Udall's gunslingers. Nine, ten months ago. I can show you where he's buried. If you got to hang me, hang me for one of them. But not for Venture."

Cabot smiled icily. "Fine. Who *did* kill Venture?"

It was on Richter's tongue, but he couldn't make himself say it. He didn't know why. Maybe it was the war—it had forged strong bonds, and he couldn't bring himself to break this last one. "Forget it," he said wearily.

Cabot laughed harshly. "That's what I thought."

The next morning they veered west, away from Glory, but Richter felt too rotten to care. They stopped after an hour and Cabot looked at him with genuine concern. "Don't worry," Richter told him. "I'll live till the hangin'."

But he no longer believed it. He felt as if he had just come to the end of a thousand-year journey, and he no longer cared what Cabot thought or did. "Listen," he said aimlessly, "just how big a pal of yours was Venture?"

"Big enough. I married his daughter."

Richter almost smiled. "So your wife's the one that sent you out on this manhunt. I thought it was more than just friendship."

Cabot colored slightly. "One way or the other. It won't make any difference to you."

"I guess not," Richter said with dim interest. "But I wonder if it would make any difference to you—if Venture turned out to be a Udall man."

Cabot went rigid. After a long, taut silence he said, "Is that what you aim to say in court?"

"It's the truth."

The Ranger's eyes became strangely reflective, as though shutters had been closed behind them. He was wondering emotionlessly if he ought to forget the court and take care of the execution himself, now.

Richter knew what he was thinking. He aimed high and took a very long shot. "I don't guess," he said, "that your wife'd like to hear a story like that in court. Even if nobody believed it."

Cabot stood rigid, his fists clinched. In theory Richter was as good as dead. But between now and the day they led him to the gallows this man was capable of making a lot of trouble in Cabot's personal life, and maybe his professional life as well.

"You could kill me now, of course," Richter told him. "Nobody'd blame you. Your wife would be satisfied. Her old man's name would stay clean. All your problems would be over. Except the one that really bothers you—the chance that I might be tellin' the truth."

The Ranger licked his thin lips. "You must want me to kill you pretty bad. Are you that scared of hangin'?"

Richter made himself grin. There was a fine bead of sweat on his forehead. "I've been wonderin' about you, Cabot. At first I pegged you as a man that could maybe do a little drygulchin' and not let it bother him. Now I don't think so."

"I wouldn't bank on that, if I was you."

Richter was suddenly tired. The old sense of hopelessness was returning. His face was hot, his vision blurred. "You're all I've got to bank on, Cabot. I don't think you'll rest before you find out if I'm lyin' about Venture."

He never heard what the Ranger said to that. Richter leaned forward a little, staring into the small fire. The next thing he knew he was looking up at the gleaming, grinning, mahogany face of Mama Sam.

Chapter Seven

They were at Mama Sam's almost a week, and the bits that Richter remembered were filled with sickness and bright with pain.

Once he awoke to find a stinking poultice plastered to his shoulder and a wet rag on his forehead. He was bunked on the dirt floor, covered with his horse blanket, and Cabot and Mama Sam were seated on crude benches, jabbering Mex at each other and drinking pulque. Richter's shoulder felt as if an invisible giant had taken hold of it and was slowly tearing the arm from the socket. Gold Tooth's knife, he guessed, hadn't been so clean, after all.

Another time he awoke to discover that he had been moved hard against the dobe wall, and the benches had been placed over him so that the wooden legs caged him in like the bars of a prison. It was night and there were perhaps a dozen Mex farm hands jammed into the small hut. A stinking tallow lamp swung from the low rafters casting bizarre, hard-edged shadows on the walls. And there was noise, a lot of noise, and what sounded like cursing in Mex, and some laughter. And in that single small room there was a shimmering aura of violence, and the sense of death, and the unmistakable sweetish smell of blood.

Later, when he came to, he thought that it had been a nightmare caused by fever. He wasn't going to mention it, but Cabot was standing over him, looking down at him with that thin grin of hatred. And Richter knew that it had been no dream.

"What happened here last night?"

"Cockfights. Mex farm hands, they work all day and gather here at night and fight their chickens. Any Mex worth the name would rather fight chickens than sleep."

That accounted for the violence that he had sensed, and the blood that he had smelled.

"Mama Sam acts as referee, and the hands give her the dead cocks when the fights are over. That's one of the ways she stays alive."

"Sounds like she's a friend of yours."

"She is. I sent her husband to prison two years ago." He saw the look on Richter's face and laughed dryly. "Mama Sam's husband tried to kill her. How do you feel?"

Richter was surprised to discover that the tearing pain in his shoulder had settled to a quiet ache. He felt sour and weak but no longer cooking with fever.

Cabot folded his arms and looked at Richter as a cowman might look at a wormy steer.

Richter said nothing. He felt no gratitude for

being alive. The hangman was still waiting in El Paso.

Mama Sam—no one seemed to know her Indian name—came in that afternoon, inspected Richter's shoulder in a brisk, businesslike manner and pronounced him cured. She gave Richter some broth of stewed gamecocks that had been killed in the night's fighting, and Cabot gave her a few pieces of silver, some tobacco, and the rest of Richter's tequila.

"We ride again tomorrow mornin'," Cabot said.

Richter said nothing.

The next morning the Ranger brought the horses around to the front of the hut. The short walk from the hut to the saddled chestnut left Richter breathless. Cabot boosted him to the high-cantled saddle and then stood glaring up at him in a kind of abstract anger.

"Mister," the Ranger said at last, "there's one thing you'd best get straight. I don't drygulch as easy as Bob Venture."

Richter looked at him blearily, too weary to wonder what he was talking about.

"And don't get the notion I won't kill you," Cabot continued. "If it comes down to that."

"The notion never entered my head," Richter told him truthfully.

"All right." Cabot mounted and they headed east. "Tell me about the Udalls."

It took Richter some time to realize that they were headed toward the mountains, away from El Paso. He turned a quick, suspicious eye on the Ranger. "Tell me about the Udalls," Cabot said for the second time.

Richter told him all that he could remember about the family; about the Udalls and the partnership; about the old man, and the son, and the coolly beautiful daughter; about Hagle and Matthews who were dead. And Tinkle who was still alive, if you could believe a hide and tallow dealer.

"But you don't want to think too hard of Tinkle," Richter heard himself saying. "You'll know what I'm talkin' about when you see Emily Udall."

Cabot grunted non-committally. Nothing that Richter had said shed any light on the murder of Bob Venture, but for the moment he let it pass.

Richter leaned forward on that big, bulbous pommel of Don Antonio's saddle, a cramp of anxiety in his gut. There had to be a point to Cabot's curiosity. There had to be a reason for their riding east instead of toward El Paso.

They rode in finely drawn silence. At last Cabot said, "Now tell me about the killin' of Bob Venture."

". . . Bushwhacked. Shot in the back by a rifleman—that's all I can tell you."

Cabot grinned unpleasantly but did not press the issue. Forced information, as he knew from experience, would be mostly lies.

They camped that night not far from the west rim of the basin. Richter was glad enough for the rest. They boiled coffee and chewed jerky, and Richter sat for a long while staring bleakly at that high wall of rock that protected the Udalls. "I take it," he said at last, "that we're headed for Glory. Would you consider tellin' me why?"

Cabot stood over him, firelight gleaming in those pale eyes. "While you was cookin' at Mama Sam's I got to thinkin' maybe I owed it to Bob Venture to prove you a liar before seein' you hang. The answer, if there is one, will be somewheres in Glory. Wouldn't you say?"

"If it's anywhere." Richter moved closer to the fire. His canvas brush jacket with no left sleeve— the sleeve was still in Jessie Marchand's hut in Prosperidad—hung grotesquely on his big frame. Somewhere along the line he had lost about twenty pounds, as well as most of his strength. But his strength was returning. A development that did not escape Cabot's notice.

"I wouldn't advise makin' a break for it," the Ranger said dryly. "You ain't in no shape yet to outrun the hangman."

But Richter was not thinking of escape. Cabot watched his prisoner like a spiraling hawk watching a fieldmouse. Richter could not understand the working of Cabot's mind, and what he didn't understand he didn't trust. "You got some kind of scheme?" he asked. "For provin' me out a liar?"

Cabot said nothing.

"You wouldn't have another pal, would you," Richter tried, "hidin' out in Glory, doin' a little spy work for you?" He could tell from Cabot's look that he was getting close. "Whoever your pal is," Richter told him, "he better have sharp ears and a fast gun hand."

Still Cabot said nothing. Richter began to like the situation less and less. What did Cabot know? There was no telling what a man might say in a fever.

Suddenly the Ranger turned from the fire, his head cocked. "Company," he said under his breath.

Now Richter heard them. Horsebackers—two of them. "Get your rig," Cabot snapped. "Move back to the gully where the horses are." He unpinned his badge and put it in his pocket.

Richter grabbed Don Antonio's heavy saddle and hurried away from the fire. He found the gully where the horses were staked and dropped the saddle, panting.

He could tell from the sound that the riders had split up and were approaching the fire from different directions. Udall hired only experienced hands; these two knew their job.

Now, peering over the lip of the gully, Richter could see them. Cabot stood arrogantly beside the fire. The two riders came toward him from right and left, rifles drawn and ready.

Cabot calmly felt for makings and began to build a smoke. "You boys make considerable racket comin' up on a man. The wages I hear Udall pays, you'd think he could hire first-class help."

The horsebackers moved into the fire's red light. Richter could see their faces now. One was dark and toothy. The other was blond, bland, and faintly grinning. Their rifles were fixed on Cabot's chest.

"Another big mouth," the fair-haired man said to his partner.

The Mex wiped the back of his hand across his mouth, his dark eyes never leaving Cabot's face. "Maybe we kill him," he said. "Not take chances."

His partner laughed. "Pedro likes it down in the basin. Plenty tequila, plenty grub, good pay. He don't like the notion of losin' his job to an outsider."

Cabot lifted one shoulder. Everybody had his problems, the shrug seemed to say. "Udall's rangin' pretty wide, ain't he? Tryin' to guard the *out*side of the basin?"

The Mex said, "I say we kill him, Drago."

The blond man looked at Pedro and spoke

sharply in Mex. Then, in English, "Udall don't want the dust stirred up. Who are you, mister?"

"Name's Cabot."

"Can you prove it?"

"Can you prove you're Drago?"

Drago laughed quietly. "I guess not. What brings you to these parts?"

"Same as brought you. And Pedro there. Good pay, good grub, good tequila."

Thoughtfully, the fair-haired man sheathed his rifle. "Scout around, Pedro. See what you can find."

"Don't spook my saddlehorse and pack animal," Cabot said. "They're back there in the gully."

Richter backed away from the lip of the gully, dragging the heavy saddle. Cabot had accounted for the two horses, now it was up to Richter to make himself invisible. He lay flat beneath an overhang of turf, a curtain of shaggy mountain grass drooping over him. He held his breath as the Mexican made a half-hearted search of the area and returned to the fire.

"Two horses," he reported. "That's all." But his rifle was still aimed at Cabot.

Drago seemed to like the Ranger's coolness. "If you're lookin' for work, might be I can help. But workin' for Udall ain't a common-run job."

"It won't be the first gun-pay I ever earned," Cabot told him.

Drago chuckled in his quiet way. "Tomorrow," he said, "come over the hump to Glory. We'll talk."

He gestured to Pedro. Reluctantly, the Mex reined his animal from the fire. The two men rode back into the night.

Cabot stood wide-legged in the dancing firelight, building a fresh smoke and lighting it. When he could no longer hear the horsebackers, he called to Richter: "Pals of yours?"

Richter came out of the dry wash and dragged his rig back to the rim of light. "I never seen them before." He gazed in the direction of Glory, and for a moment he glimpsed the two riders silhouetted against the dark skyline, apparently making a routine patrol of the major approaches to the pass. Nevertheless, he was careful to stay well away from the fire.

"This a common thing with Udall?" Cabot asked. "Settin' a guard outside the basin?"

"It wasn't when I was a part of the outfit. He must be pretty spooky."

"What would spook a man like Udall?"

"Maybe just knowin' I'm still alive. In spite of the considerable trouble he's gone to to get me buried."

Cabot grunted non-committally. He went on about the business of securing the camp, just as though he were alone. Back in the darkness and brush Richter threw his roll.

"Cabot?"

Cabot moved a hissing coffeepot away from the fire. "What?"

"You aim to meet that hand of Udall's tomorrow. In Glory?"

"That's why we come this way, ain't it?"

"I wasn't sure. But Udall's no fool. If he guesses you might be a Ranger he'll kill you on the spot and feed you to the coyotes."

Cabot made a dry sound in his throat. "Back across the Bravo you had me pegged for a hired killer. So did that barkeep pal of yours. And the cantina girl. Now it looks like Drago thinks the same thing. I figger I can make Udall swallow it . . . for a while, anyhow."

"What if you run into somebody that knows you?"

The Ranger made that sound again. "That would be hard luck for me," he said dryly, "and good luck for you."

The fire burned low. Cabot threw his blanket and kicked out the live coals. A pale moon in its final quarter appeared. A long silence settled on that broken land.

Perhaps an hour passed. Perhaps longer. Richter lay wide-eyed, painfully awake, running the situation through his mind and trying, without luck, to make sense of it.

He didn't like the notion of meekly turning his life over to the care of a stranger, and more especially a stranger who had arrested him for murder. But he had considered the possibility of escape and had not found it promising. There was only one way to make an escape work; he would have to kill the Ranger. And killing a Ranger was never a simple matter. He did not consider it seriously.

For the thousandth time he tried to guess what Cabot was up to. Why had he switched from his attitude of hostility and extreme caution?

"Cabot?" The word came suddenly, unexpectedly.

The Ranger answered immediately. "What?"

Richter smiled, relieved to know that Cabot's transformation had not been so complete, after all. If he had been sleeping, it had been with one eye open and a gun in his hand. But Richter knew that he had not been sleeping. He had been waiting patiently, for Richter to ask his question.

Richter said slowly, "How come you all of a sudden begin to trust me?"

Richter could almost see that humorless smile. "Two reasons, if you got to know," Cabot said. "For one thing, there ain't anywheres you can run that I won't find you. I figger you know that."

"The other reason?"

"The girl," Cabot said casually. "The Marchand woman that you knew in Prosperidad. She's in Glory now."

Richter sat bolt upright. His sudden anger didn't seem to surprise Cabot, but it surprised Richter. "Jessie Marchand's got nothin' to do with this!"

"Jessie Marchand seems to think different," the Ranger said. "While you was at Mama Sam's stewin' with fever, I rode back across the Bravo and told her how it was with you. And how it was goin' to be." He sighed. "I told her how you was goin' to hang, without you found a way to prove your story about the way Bob Venture was killed. Well—it ain't for me to say what's right and what's wrong for a woman that's come through the things she has. But I'll say this for her, she's got a good head on her shoulders. She saw right off that, in a town like Glory, a stranger would have next to no chance at all of gettin' the straight of things. But a saloon woman . . ." He let the word hang for a moment. "Saloon women— one way or another they hear everything."

Richter unclamped his jaw with some difficulty. "She's in Glory now?"

"Unless she was lyin' about wantin' to help you. And I don't think she was."

"I guess you know," Richter grated, "that you put her in a first-class way of gettin' herself killed."

"I know. And so does she."

Richter got a sudden glimpse at the intricate working of Cabot's mind. "You knowed from

163

the first that I wasn't the one that killed your pal, Venture!"

Somewhere in the darkness Cabot shrugged unconcernedly. Richter could almost see him. "I didn't know it. And I still don't. Just say that I come around to agreein' that it *could* of been somebody else . . . and consider yourself lucky."

Richter called him an ugly name.

Cabot only grunted.

Chapter Eight

L ittle more than one year old, the town seemed already in the last stages of old age. The sorry, greenwood structures were twisted and faded and leaning precariously with the wind. Tumbleweeds trundled forlornly the length of Main Street with no man or vehicle to deter them. The only person in sight was a storekeeper who had stepped out to the dirt walk to dash a bucket of refuse into the street. He eyed the approaching horsebacker without interest and went back into the plank shack that called itself a general store.

Winter lay softly on the sheltered basin floor, though a dazzling sun gave surprisingly little heat. Cabot, riding Don Antonio's Thoroughbred and leading his own animal, reined up at the watering trough at the head of the street and let the animals drink.

Ritcher had been uneasy and more than slightly bitter about being left afoot and unarmed in hostile country. But, in Cabot's book, Richter was still his prisoner and possibly the murderer of Bob Venture. He had left him in a way that would make him easy enough to find later.

So Cabot had entered the town alone, a little past midday; alone and unnoticed, so it had seemed at first. But soon after entering the basin he had glimpsed the dull gleam of metal among the high formations of rock that overlooked the pass—the gleam of blue gunsteel reflecting winter sunlight. The entrance to Udall's tight little principality wasn't quite as welcoming as it would first appear.

On the sheer slopes of the western wall Cabot could see the half-finished but imposing structure that was to be the Udall castle. Riding across the basin floor he had seen the Udall herds thriving on a table of gravel and brown grass. Udall's cattle, with Udall's huge Mexican brand on their sides. A stranger would never have guessed that this had ever been anything but Udall's basin.

At the far end of the street there was a fragile shed and a rawhide corral that passed as a livery outfit of sorts. Cabot counted three horses in the corral. Somewhere, out of sight, a blacksmith worked half-heartedly at his anvil.

At the moment the only sign of life was three horses burdened with Mex rocking chair saddles, dozing at a rack in front of a death-gray structure next door to the general store. A swinging, squeaking, already-peeling sign over the door announced without enthusiasm that this was the GLORY CAFE AND BAR.

Jessie Marchand was sitting at a table with two Udall vaqueros when Cabot came in. She turned and gazed disinterestedly at Cabot, laughing at something one of the vaqueros had said. The

Glory Cafe and Bar was one large, starkly naked rectangle with four plank tables and a sawhorse bar. There was a glowing iron cookstove in the back. The heated air of the place was heavily laced with the eye-watering aromas of chili, garlic, sour beer, and burning cowchips.

A Mex woman with a face the shape and color of a plump, ripe persimmon, watched Cabot from behind the plank bar. Cabot pointed at a bottle and said, "Whiskey." He put a silver dollar on the bar and the woman stared at it with suspicion. "We use Glory money here," she said in Spanish.

The woman showed him a square of paper, about half the size of a common greenback. It was scrip—Udall scrip—worth one dollar silver. So it claimed.

"I just landed here," Cabot told her. "I haven't got any scrip."

Muttering to herself, the woman poured his drink and took the silver, reluctantly. In change she gave him three squares of pasteboard, each claiming the value of one quarter of one dollar. Cabot was beginning to understand how Henry Udall had got to be a rich man.

The whiskey was drinkable, but at a quarter a shot it was no bargain. Cabot spent another piece of pasteboard and took the glass to a table. Jessie Marchand was still laughing and drinking with the vaqueros. She didn't look his way again.

Cabot nursed his whiskey. A giant of a man

wearing a stocking cap and a leather black-smith's apron came in and said something to the woman barkeep. The woman went back to the cookstove and soon the smell of chili and garlic overwhelmed all other smells in the room.

The blacksmith drank the still, pale beer while his food was being prepared. He turned and looked steadily at Cabot with an impersonal, inactive hatred. Then the woman brought his plate and he ate at the bar, fried beans and boiled green chilis and thick tortillas. Then, with another look at Cabot, he settled his debt in pasteboard and left.

Almost immediately the door opened and another customer entered the combination eating house–saloon. Cabot was beginning to think that Glory was not as lifeless as outside appearances had led him to believe.

The Ranger studied the new customer with interest. Obviously, from the way the barwoman jumped to serve him, he was a man of some importance. "Whiskey," he said with a short-tempered edge to his voice.

Cabot gazed with surprise and appreciation at the bottle of old Tennessee whiskey that appeared on the bar. The man filled a whiskey glass and drained it. He stood very still for perhaps half a minute, then he filled the glass again and poured it down. Only then did he direct any attention at all to the other people in the room.

He wore an expensive-looking suit of hard worsted that had been carefully fitted to his lanky frame. Cabot studied the long face, the weak eyes, the lines of worry—the face of an overworked schoolmaster. Or a prosperous undertaker. Or a hell-fire preacher that had lost his faith. He did not wear a gun. Cabot had never seen him before, but somehow he knew that this was Tinkle, the last member of the original partnership still in Glory.

He slapped the bar with his hand, and the sound was startling. The room had become very still and quiet. The woman barkeep jumped to refill the empty glass, but Jessie Marchand and the two vaqueros sat perfectly still, staring at one another with wooden faces.

Tinkle looked at the party at the table, his lip curled with contempt. He downed his third drink. But not his third of the day. Cabot realized that the man was quite drunk. Not staggering drunk, not rowdy drunk, but mean and dangerous, in his own quiet way.

He turned his sneering attention to Cabot, noting the trail-dirty clothing, the carefully cared-for revolver and holster. Suddenly he smiled, and the smile was uglier than the sneer.

"I don't remember seein' *your* face before."

Cabot looked at him and shrugged.

Tinkle seemed to go up in a blaze of anger. "Goddamn you, answer me when I speak to you!"

Cabot felt the heat rush to his face, but he sat perfectly still and said mildly, "You never seen my face because I never showed it around here before."

The unruffled response seemed to enrage Tinkle further, but the form of his anger changed from hot to coldly calculating. He held out his glass and the woman filled it immediately. "Gunhands," he said, as if the word had been dragged through slime. He moved toward Cabot, stepping out with the extreme caution of an experienced drunkard. He paused in front of Cabot, smiling his thin, unpleasant smile. Without a hint of warning, he dashed the whiskey in Cabot's face.

Cabot sat like stone. With a knot in his gut and ire in his brain, and that fine old Tennessee whiskey dripping from his chin and bringing tears to his eyes. But he sat like stone and did not make a sound. The Glory Cafe and Bar held its breath.

The front door burst open. Drago and his worried-looking Mex partner burst into the electric stillness, their revolvers in their hands. Both men were clearly shaken. They paused just inside the doorway, their guns trained as if by magic on Cabot's chest. Cabot did not look at them. He didn't even look at Tinkle. He sat perfectly still with whiskey dripping off his chin.

"Set where you are, mister," Drago said to Cabot. He crossed the floor quickly, as if he were walking on live coals. "There's doin's up at the big house," he said, moving like a shadow between Tinkle and Cabot. "Mr. Udall," he said to Tinkle, "wants to see you."

Tinkle's smile widened. "You were almost too late this time, Drago. You know how Mr. Udall feels about havin' his friends gunned down on Main Street. You're supposed to watch out for me. Ain't that what he told you?"

Both Drago and Pedro were sweating freely. "Please," Drago said—a strange-sounding word in a gunman's mouth—"we're supposed to bring you up to the big house."

Tinkle laughed. He allowed the empty glass to drop from his fingers, and it rattled noisily across the floor. Gingerly, Pedro took his arm. Surprisingly, Tinkle allowed himself to be led toward the door. Drago, with a quick, icy glance at Cabot, said, "Set right there, mister. I'll be back in a little while."

As suddenly as it had started, it was over. Tinkle and Drago and Pedro were gone. The door closed behind them. Slowly, Cabot lifted his arm and wiped his face on his sleeve.

The woman barkeep became suddenly very busy with her stove. The two vaqueros got up and headed for the door. The big sunburst rowels of their spurs made an unnerving clamor in the room.

Cabot waited for his mouth to become a little

less dry, his muscles a little less cramped. Then he turned and looked at Jessie Marchand and said, "Bring me a bottle."

She laughed, but the sound was strained. "I guess you got somethin' to celebrate, at that. Just bein' alive." She went behind the bar, got a bottle of regular bar whiskey and brought it to the table with a glass for herself. The Mex woman was still at the stove working off her jitters.

"That was a near thing," Jessie Marchand said quietly, taking a chair beside the Ranger. "You know who that was? The one so free and easy with his whiskey?"

"Richter's old pard, Tinkle?"

She nodded, looking only slightly surprised. "I've been here three days and you're the third 'gunslinger' he's tried to get a rise out of."

"Is he always like that? Drunk?"

She nodded again. "And a little crazy too, I think. He's got the Udalls bothered. I mean, the way he keeps rubbin' hardcases the wrong way— like he was *tryin'* to get himself killed. Or maybe it's just to rile the Udalls. Usually Drago's on hand to watch out for him."

"Why would the Udalls worry about keeping him alive?"

She shook her head. "I don't know. There are a lot of things about this place I don't know." She looked down at her drink. ". . . How's Richter?"

Cabot told her about the spell of fever and

Mama Sam. "But he's on the mend. Don't worry about him."

Her smile was strangely sad. "Why should I worry about him?"

"I don't know. Maybe because he's worryin' about you."

She looked at the Ranger in a strange, shy way. She wanted to believe him. But half a year in the mountains with Pepe Groz and his bandits had conditioned her not to believe too much in the word of men. Sometimes she thought that she must be a little loco herself, allowing herself to listen to Cabot in the first place, risking her life for a bull-headed nobody like Richter. For she had learned one thing during her three-day stay in Glory. Udall was a man who had to have his own way. He hadn't hired a gunslinger like Drago, or his Mex pal, because they were handy with cattle.

She said, "I heard some of Udall's vaqueros talking. They don't think I know but a few words of Mex, so they talk free enough when I'm around. Anyhow . . . Udall's put a bounty on Richter's scalp."

"There's nothin' new about that. If you believe Richter's side of the story."

She shook her head. "This is different. Before, he was just sendin' hired guns across the Bravo, hopin' they'd get a chance to gun Richter down with as little fuss as possible. Now nobody seems

173

very interested in how much fuss they make. Udall just wants to see Richter's hide curing in the sun. If you ask me, I think he's scared."

"Of Richter?"

"Of something."

Cabot thought for a moment. "What have you heard about the killing of Bob Venture?"

"They say Richter did it, but I don't think anybody really believes it. But they have to say it. That way, the man that guns Richter and collects the bounty works out to be a public-spirited citizen instead of a murderer. Everybody's in on it. The Mex farmers, the vaqueros, storekeepers."

"How much bounty has Udall put up?"

"Five thousand gold, I heard a vaquero say."

Cabot whistled. "The Udalls must want him pretty bad. And they must know that Richter's headed back toward Glory. With even cow-hands and farmers lookin' forward to a piece of the bounty." He smiled coldly. "And that's a notion that I don't rest too easy with. If they know about Richter, might be they know about you, too."

She returned his humorless smile. "And you," she said.

They looked at each other. "Maybe I oughtn't to of brought you here."

She shrugged. "I'd had a bait of Prosperidad." She poured a drink and downed it quickly.

The door swung open and Drago and the

Mexican came directly to their table. Cabot said, "I hope your whiskey-wastin' friend is put away safe for a spell."

Drago grunted. "I been tellin' Mr. Udall how you set there and let Tinkle pitch Tennessee bourbon in your face and didn't kill him. Mr. Udall liked that. Self-control, he calls it. Mr. Udall sets great store in self-control."

"So do prison guards. This Tinkle—he a pal of Udall's?"

Drago hesitated. "You might call him that." He shrugged the matter away. "You still lookin' for a job?"

"I could use the money."

"All right." Drago jerked his head toward the door. "You come with me and Pedro."

Suddenly things were moving too fast for comfort. Cabot needed more time to talk to Jessie Marchand and to get the feel of things. He didn't like the notion of being suddenly tied to a job, letting a prisoner run loose on the other side of the pass.

But Drago, or Udall, had taken the play out of his hands. He went to the bar and paid for what was gone from the bottle and got his change in pasteboard. Suddenly he could think of any number of questions that he should have put to Jessie Marchand and hadn't. It was too late now. He turned toward the table, and she smiled with saloon girl weariness and saluted with her glass.

Cabot looked at Udall's two gunhands. "I'm ready if you are."

Udall's big house was not nearly completed, but Cabot was impressed by what he saw. The foundations had been dug for a house that would be even larger than Don Antonio's ancestral home when it was finished. Huge thirty-inch thick adobe blocks were stood in ordered lines along the slope, slowly curing in the winter sun. Other buildings and sheds had been laid out. Perhaps twenty Mexican laborers scurried up and down that slope, mixing adobe, digging postholes, trenching foundations and carrying rock.

Drago led the way beneath an unfinished gallery, through a doorless entranceway and along a roofless and ceilingless hallway. They turned into a great, unfinished room where a taut, hawklike dude was brandishing a silver-headed cane at a laborer who was attempting to set the keystone in what would one day be a cavernous fireplace. He wheeled and glared at Cabot with feverish eyes, then gestured impatiently with the cane and the laborer vanished.

"You call yourself Cabot?"

Cabot nodded. There was no doubt in his mind that this man was Henry Udall.

Udall lifted his chin, sniffing with his hawkish nose, as if the scent of something unclean had drifted through the topless room. "Is it true that you sat like a wart on a toad while a drunken nobody dashed whiskey in your face?"

Cabot was aware that there must be a sound method to Udall's sneering tone. All the same, his face warmed, and the buttoned collar of his shirt felt suddenly tight. But when he spoke it was with no trace of emotion. "Your man Drago told you about it. Don't you believe him?"

"I'm asking you," Udall snapped.

Cabot shrugged. "The dude was unarmed. So I sat there and took it. Besides, rigged out the way he was, I figgered maybe he was a Udall."

Henry Udall raised one dark eyebrow. He somehow managed to smile and sneer in one expression. "Maybe," he said, as though he doubted it. "Or maybe you're simply gutless, or stupid. Probably both."

"If you believe that, I rode a long piece out of my way for nothin'."

The hawkish face turned thoughtful. He looked sharply at Drago.

"He was there," the gunhand said, "in the same place, when we went back. Talkin' to that new saloon girl I told you about."

"Well," Udall said quietly, almost to himself, "we'll see." He looked a silent order at the Mex. Pedro wheeled and loped out of the room, leaving a racket of jangling spurs behind him.

A quiet, insidious chill crawled like some long,

pale worm in Cabot's gut. Something here was not right. Udall was not the kind of man to stew over whether to hire or not to hire a common gunhand.

"Look here," Cabot started. But Udall stopped him with a raised hand and a chilly smile. Drago waited with a wooden face, ready, on Udall's command, to jump in any direction. And the worm behind Cabot's belt buckle crawled deeper.

Once again they heard the clamor of Pedro's spurs, and the Mex blundered down the stone-floored hallway and into the unfinished room. He nodded to Udall, and Udall merely blinked and waited a few seconds longer in silence.

Now someone else was coming down the hallway. Suddenly Cabot realized that Drago and Pedro had moved in quite close, on either side of him. Then a smooth, dark face peered in from the hallway. A face that looked at Cabot with instant fury—and then, just as instantly, was grinning widely, many yellow teeth gleaming like wet ivory. Cabot had no trouble recognizing him. His name was Juan Gomez, pal of the young knife-throwing Mex that Richter had killed in Prosperidad.

Juan moved into the room and pointed dramatically at Cabot. "He's the one!"

By that time it was much too late for Cabot to think of fighting his way out. Drago and Pedro had already grabbed his arms in steel-trap grips.

For the moment all the Ranger's anger was directed at himself. He should have remembered that Richter had mentioned the Udalls to this grinning killer. He should have guessed that Juan Gomez would not give up his vendetta so easily but would quickly track the Udall name to Glory.

Juan was enjoying himself hugely. Not only would he have his revenge, he would be a rich man if he collected the bounty. He stepped up to the helpless Ranger, chuckling, and Cabot made a grave mistake. He lunged against the restraining arms of the gunhands. Quickly, quietly, and without fuss, Udall lashed out with the heavy silver head of his cane.

"All in good time," Udall snapped. His voice was edged. Some of the arrogance seemed to have drained out of it. "First we've got to know what brought him here. And what he did with Richter. What else did you find in his pockets?"

Drago answered. "Not much. A pocketknife, matches, a sack of makin's. No money except for a Mex peso and the scrip he picked up at the bar." The gunhand sounded amused. "Maybe we could make a deal with him."

"Don't talk like a fool," Udall said coldly.

"You had a deal with the other one, didn't you? The one called Venture."

"Venture was no Ranger. Any out-of-work

nester with nothing better to do can manage a deputy marshal's job. A Ranger is a different proposition."

The words sank slowly into Cabot's consciousness. His head throbbed. He felt sick, but not from the pain. He had liked Bob Venture, not just because he was his father-in-law, he had liked him as a man. But flesh is weak. And the temptation of money, to a man trying to raise a family on a deputy marshal's pay, must have been strong. He sighed involuntarily. A sadness wrapped itself around him like a winding sheet.

"He's coming around," Udall said.

Drago turned Cabot over with the toe of his boot, the way he would turn over a dead coyote. "Come alive, Ranger. The play party's over."

Now Cabot saw that they were in a lean-to addition to a larger structure. Originally, he guessed, it was meant to be a tack room, for various pieces of riding gear still hung on the wall, side by side with sacked bacon.

There were no windows in the room; on the front wall a lighted lantern hung on a nail. Drago and Pedro stood on either side of Cabot, relaxed but ready for anything. Udall was thoughtfully fondling the Ranger's badge.

Cabot sat up, slowly, his head pounding. He fixed Udall with a pale-eyed stare. "That's some walkin' stick you got."

Udall smiled his chilly smile. "Tell me," he said conversationally, "what brings a Texas Ranger to a quiet little hamlet like Glory?"

Cabot considered several stories but discarded all of them. Better to keep them guessing. It was beginning to look as if his life was pegged on the single nail of Udall's curiosity. When that was satisfied, there would no longer be a reason for keeping him alive.

Udall shrugged his stooped shoulders. "Pedro here once lived among the Yaquis and learned their ways. I'm sure he could persuade you to tell us whatever we might want to know."

Cabot knew about the Yaquis. Not even the tortures of the Kiowas could compete with Yaquis' centuries of experience in such matters. Cabot glanced up at Pedro's brown face. Pedro grinned.

Cabot pretended to be unmoved, knowing that the man had not been born who could out-last more than a few minutes of serious Yaqui attention. "You know how it is," he said. "A man with his brains simmerin' over a low fire will say anything."

Udall nodded slightly. "Nevertheless . . ."

Cabot considered. From Juan Gomez they already knew about his taking Richter prisoner, so he said, "I guess you want to know where Richter is . . ."

Udall's expression told him that he had guessed

181

right. Drago and the Mex looked surprised, but Udall showed a slight tightening of parchment-like skin over jutting cheekbones. "We know that you took Richter from our young friend here. And some of my farm hands heard from some Mexican cockfighters that you and a man of Richter's description laid over a week or so at an old woman's called Mama Sam. But when Drago and Pedro raised your camp last night, you were alone . . . Or were you?"

"If I hadn't been, I reckon Drago would of mentioned it to you."

"It was nighttime. Richter could have been hiding."

"Could have." Cabot shrugged. "But wasn't. Half a day out of Mama Sam's he escaped . . ." They didn't believe him. Cabot forced himself to grin. "Richter's got a way with him, when it comes to escapin'. You ought to know, Udall. He got away from you, didn't he? And he got away from a deputy U. S. Marshal."

Drago and Pedro went suddenly blank. Cabot imagined that Udall's yellowish face grew a little paler. The self-styled lord of Glory nodded slowly. "Did he tell you about his escape from the marshal?"

"Just that Venture got careless, and Richter killed him."

Obviously Udall wanted to believe him. But he didn't. He took a deep breath and sighed. "Which brings us back to the point of this talk. What, exactly, brings a Ranger to Glory?"

"I already told you." He paused. "The only thing I know about Richter, besides the fact that he murdered Marshal Venture, was that he hated your guts and was determined to settle accounts with you before he hung."

Udall cleared his throat—his first outward show of nerves. "Well, we'll soon know. I've sent riders to talk to Mama Sam." He smiled, and Cabot got the feeling that most of the "talking" would be done with knife-steel and leather quirts. "And of course," Udall added, "I'll inspect the camp where you spent the night. If you had company, I'll know."

Cabot licked his cracked lips and grimly told himself that he never should have listened to Richter in the first place. He would have done them both a favor if he had simply taken Richter to El Paso and hung him. Then another disturbing possibility crossed his mind. What if Juan Gomez wandered into Glory's bar-cafe and saw Jessie Marchand? It wouldn't take him long to match her up with Richter.

Udall suddenly took a brisk, businesslike attitude, nodding to his gunhands. "Tie him up. See that nothing happens to him . . . until we learn just where we stand."

Pedro made another of his noisy trips outside and soon returned with two lengths of rope. He and Drago bound Cabot's hands and feet. Udall started for the door.

"I wonder . . ." Cabot said quietly, and Udall paused for a moment in the doorway. "I wonder if you ever heard of anybody gettin' away with killin' a Ranger."

Udall looked as if he might smile, but didn't. "No. But then, no one ever got away with crossing a Udall, either."

Cabot lay in darkness—Drago had blown out the lantern before leaving him alone. He sawed at the ropes on his hands and feet. His efforts only rubbed the skin raw and made his head pound. He lay for a long while, panting. Then, as he was about to try again, the door to the shed swung open.

Cold moonlight poured across the floor. A tall, hunched figure, backlighted by the moon, swayed in the doorway. Although Cabot could not see his face, the Ranger knew that he was once again looking at Richter's old pal, Tinkle. Even before Tinkle stepped inside the storeroom Cabot smelled his whiskey breath.

"I've got to talk to you, Ranger." He sounded as sober as a coldwater Baptist preacher, but Cabot noticed that he carefully grasped both sides of the door frame before attempting an entrance. He stood against the rectangle of moonlight, staring down at the helpless Ranger. "I've got to know," he said heavily. "Where's Richter?"

Several cruel replies darted through Cabot's mind, but he determinedly ignored them. After a moment's silence he asked, "Why?"

"If Udall's men find him, they'll kill him. I want to help him."

"The way you helped him before?" Cabot could not mask the contempt that he felt. "I don't think so, Tinkle. Wherever Richter is, he'll stand a better chance against Udall's men than he would against you."

Tinkle sighed. He stood in profile against the pale light. He drew a revolver, appeared to study the weapon for a moment, and then he bent over Cabot and laid the cold steel of the barrel alongside the Ranger's cheek. "You know where Richter is, and you'll tell me." He tapped the barrel against Cabot's cheekbone.

"So you're the old pal Richter told me about," Cabot said, each word tipped with gall. "Went through the war together. Old pards, through thick and thin."

Tinkle swung the revolver in a deceptively offhanded way. For a moment Cabot was numbed by the shock. He felt his cheek burst. He tasted blood in his mouth and felt blood flowing warmly down into the collar of his shirt.

"I never come here to hash over old times," Tinkle told him slowly, forming each word with drunken preciseness.

Cabot turned his head and spat blood.

"Now what about Richter?" Tinkle reminded him. "You want to tell me where he's at?"

"I might be tempted to tell you," Cabot said, more puzzled than angered, "if I knew. And if I thought you might explain why it was so important."

"It's not hard to understand . . ." A third voice had disturbed the air of quiet, sardonic violence.

Cabot squirmed so that he could see the second of his visitors. A sulphur match flared, as startling as ignited flashpowder. In that harsh, sudden light Tinkle seemed to shrink visibly. The girl who stepped into the littered storeroom could only have been Emily Udall.

She went directly to the hanging lantern, raised the chimney and put the match to the wick. All the time her eyes never left Tinkle's face, and her contempt for him was withering. Cabot could have been another sack of corn meal or crate of canned goods, for all the attention she paid him.

"Tinkle," she said acidly, flicking away the burned-out match, "has been a cruel disappointment to all of us. At the moment I can hardly believe it, but there was a time when I had high hopes for him . . ." Her face was a perfect oval and every bit as beautiful as Richter had described it. She wore a black whipcord riding dress and carried a leather crop—from time to time she would run her fingers along the

186

length of braided leather, reminding Cabot of a professional assassin fondly caressing his favorite weapon.

She moved casually to the opposite wall and then returned, studying Tinkle from all angles, and finding none of them to her liking. "As for the others," she said, "none of them ever amounted to anything. Matthews—a great red-faced bull and a bumbling idiot. Richter—a common saddle tramp. Hagle . . ." Here she paused, as if momentarily surprised to hear the name spoken. She frowned slightly, strangely puzzled and shocked by the memories that rushed through her mind. "Hagle," she said again, softly. "A baby. A gangling colt . . ." She could not bring herself to admit out loud that Hagle had also been her husband.

By the second, as Emily Udall stared at him, Tinkle seemed to grow smaller and smaller. He licked his dry lips, desperately sober, much too sober for his own good. "Emily, I had to find out," he said huskily. "If Richter's back, if he's out there somewheres, there's no tellin' what mischief he'll stir up . . ."

She smiled fiercely—an ugly crack appearing suddenly on a porcelain face. "Go back to your bottle—it's the only friend you've got left."

Before her taunting he was diminished to a shadow of a man. His hands began to tremble. He couldn't look at her; he couldn't even look at Cabot. "You'll treat me with respect," he mumbled. "I'm as good as the Udalls. Good as anybody. You know what would happen if . . ."

Her lip curled. She snarled in anger. "Get away! I don't want to look at you!"

Tinkle's tongue flicked along his dry lips. Her strength and her anger were too much for him. He ducked his head and, with a curious sidling movement, slipped across the floor and out the door. He disappeared, like a shadow disappearing with the coming of darkness.

Cabot had observed the bizarre scene with acute interest but with little understanding. He looked at Emily Udall, studying her face and eyes intently, and his rapt attention seemed to anger her. "I take it," he said slowly, "that Richter's old pal ain't exactly a favorite of yours."

"Tinkle . . ." She gestured angrily with the riding crop. "He's a fool, and a drunkard. He's nothing."

"I'd about figgered that out myself. What devils me is why the Udalls put up with him and protect him. Not because of the water rights—you would have figgered a way to get *them* away from him, by this time."

She frowned and, for the first time, seemed to recognize the danger that this Ranger presented. She wheeled, facing the open doorway, and stared out at the night.

Cabot became aware of the silence that extended outside the storeroom. "Sounds empty out there. Everybody out scoutin' for Richter?"

She nodded automatically, her mind somewhere else. Then she looked sharply at the Ranger. "Do you know where he is? Richter?" She gestured impatiently. "If they find him . . . Something might happen."

Cabot stared, then he laughed abruptly. Only after he had studied her expression of anger did he realize that it was just possible that she didn't know everything that her brother and father knew. "Somethin'll happen, all right," he said. "They'll kill him."

"If he tries to fight them, they will."

Cabot shook his head. "Kill him. Plain and simple. Any way they can. The way they killed Matthews, and Hagle, and anybody else that gets in their way."

In the flickering lantern light her face looked dead.

"That's a lie! Hagle and Matthews—that was an accident."

Did she actually believe that? She herself had set up the double killing, according to Richter.

"Think about it," Cabot said quietly, almost gently. "Think about the way it happened, and why. Then tell me if it was an accident."

But somewhere in her past she had learned the trick of shutting unpleasant thoughts out of her mind, and she used it now. "What could you know about it?" she snapped.

"Only what Richter told me. And the longer I lay here bound hand and feet, the easier it is to believe everything he said."

Her lip curled again. "Richter is a fool."

"But a dangerous one, for the Udalls. And whatever the Udalls find dangerous, the Udalls kill. Ain't that the size of it?"

She stared thin-lipped but said nothing.

"While we're on the subject," Cabot said dryly, "what do you figger your pa and your brother and your gunhands have got in mind for me. You don't think they'll let me go, do you?"

She wheeled abruptly and faced the open doorway, but did not leave the storeroom. "Ma'am," he drawled in that tone of false gentility, "it might just be that the Udalls could have a few Mex vaqueros killed, and blame it on Richter, and get away with it. It might even be that they could arrange to have a pair of nobodies like Hagle and Matthews kill each other. And a saddle tramp like Richter—a man wanted for murder—they could put an end to him with no trouble at all. Comin' down to cases, they might even get away with killin' a government deputy like Bob Venture." He paused to let the meaning of the words make an impression. Then he said, "But not a Ranger. When a Ranger dies other Rangers want to know how and why and all about it."

He could not see her face, but she stood ramrod-straight, clutching the riding crop with both hands. "You might want to think it over," he said, "before the menfolks get back. You might just be doin' them a favor if you untied me and let me go."

She waited several seconds before replying. "Do you think I'm a fool!"

"No ma'am. That's why I brought the subject up."

She gripped the crop harder. "Nothing will happen to you, Ranger. Tinkle . . . sometimes he does crazy things when he's drunk. But I stopped him, didn't I?"

"That was you, not your pa or brother."

She slammed out of the storeroom, bolting the door on the outside.

Chapter Nine

Since early afternoon Richter had been watching those high, brush-grown hills for some sign of the Ranger. He understood that it could take days, or even weeks, for Cabot and Jessie Marchand to uncover anything that would be useful. But that didn't stop him from watching expectantly and growing edgy when Cabot did not appear.

Between fits of impatience he cursed the Ranger for leaving him afoot and unarmed, but most of all he was angered at Cabot for bringing Jessie Marchand into all this. Being responsible for a cantina girl had never been part of the bargain.

The day died quietly, without a murmur. Richter hunkered in the gray dusk, fireless, chewing on some jerky that Cabot had left with him. He had moved to higher ground, in a thicket of catclaw, overlooking the campsite of the night before.

With the sun gone a penetrating chill settled on those rugged slopes of the high Chanattes. Richter wrapped himself in one of Cabot's blankets but did not consider the possibility of sleep. Maybe it was the silence, the lifelessness of the mountains, that seemed to raise sensitive nerve ends to the surface of his skin. Maybe it was the aftereffects of infection and fever, but most likely it was simply the awareness of being so close to Glory and the Udalls and not being able to do a thing about it.

So he waited, alone, beneath the thornbrush which seemed to glow dully in the gathering darkness, like a tangle of spiked bones.

The night was getting colder. Richter found a threadbare place in the blanket and made a foot-long slit. He pulled the blanket over him, forcing his head through the hole, and wore it like a poncho. While he was doing this some horsebackers had come up from the lower slope.

Richter froze. He counted the sounds—four horsemen—and they seemed to be making for the camp that he had deserted.

"You're sure this is the place?" someone asked. Richter sucked in his breath, recognizing Giles Udall's voice.

He picked out another voice. "This is the place, all right." The Udall gunhand, Drago. "No sign of life, best I can see. It's just the way the Ranger would of left it."

Ranger. Richter's insides fell. So they knew about Cabot; knew that he was a Ranger, anyway. Well, Richter thought angrily, *that* didn't take long!

A third voice muttered something in Mex—Pedro, Drago's shadow. Then Drago said, "Maybe the Ranger's tellin' it straight. Maybe

193

this Richter we're lookin' for got away from him."

Giles Udall laughed. It was not a pleasant sound.

They scouted the area a while longer, two of them dismounted. Suddenly Pedro snapped some sort of warning in Mex, and Giles cursed angrily. "Why didn't you tell me about this gully!"

There was a moment of comparative silence. One of the riders seemed to be moving back and forth between the campsite and the gully, as if he were thoughtfully measuring the distance. Finally the fourth rider spoke. This time it was none other than the lord of Glory himself, Henry Udall.

"That's where he was," he said coldly, without a trace of doubt in his voice. "There in the gully, right under your noses."

Pedro objected strenuously in Mex. Drago broke in quickly, "There wasn't nobody but the Ranger when we was here. Pedro scouted up and down the gully; there wasn't nobody there, just the two horses."

"*Two* horses," Henry Udall said, his tone as flat as the broad side of a saber.

Of course, there might have been any number of reasons why a person would travel cross-country with two horses, but none of these reasons pleased the master of Glory. "Search the gully again," he snapped.

194

From his place beneath the bony branches of the thorn tree, Richter watched the two dark shapes of Giles and Henry Udall. After a while the two gunhands returned from the gully. "A saddle," Drago said apologetically. "A heavy Mex rig. Lot of silver."

Richter could almost see Henry Udall smiling coldly. "A Mexican saddle. Didn't that boy—Gomez—say that a rich bull raiser had fitted Richter out with a horse and riding rig?"

There was a note of worry, as well as anger, in Drago's voice. "The Ranger was lyin'. Richter *was* here with him. But he come into Glory by hisself. One way or other Richter must of talked hisself out of the trip to El Paso. Too bad." The gunhand sighed. "For the Ranger."

"Too bad for *us,*" Giles Udall said angrily. "If we don't find Richter before he starts telling everything he knows or suspects."

"Who would believe him—a renegade, wanted for killin' a government lawman?"

"Maybe nobody would believe him," Giles snarled. "But a lot of people would listen when he told about a missing Ranger."

Henry Udall said in his coldly offhanded way, "Shut up, both of you. What's done is done. Our problem is simple—Richter has been wounded, and he's afoot, and possibly unarmed. He can't have traveled far. In the morning I'll put all available hands to looking for him."

"And if they don't find him?" Giles asked uneasily.

Once again Richter got the feeling that the dark shape in the modified stovepipe hat was smiling. "If we don't find Richter, we'll let Richter find us."

The horsebackers were gone, had been gone for an hour or more, and Richter still crouched in the thicket of thorns. The chill of the night crept into his bones, and the blanket poncho didn't seem to help. His teeth began to chatter. His shoulder ached. He began to be sorry that he had ever left Don Antonio's generous bed and board.

Gomez . . . Udall had mentioned the name. Somebody called Gomez had known that Don Antonio had furnished Richter with horse and rig. But he couldn't remember anybody by the name of Gomez. He scarcely remembered Gold Tooth himself, sprawled dead on a manure pile in Prosperidad.

The thing that bothered Richter was something else that Henry Udall had said. *"If we don't find Richter, we'll let Richter find us."*

Udall knew his man. Better, perhaps, than Richter knew himself.

There's just one thing to do, he thought. Get away from here. Away from Glory, away from Texas.

Once he got back across the Bravo, Don

Antonio could somehow smuggle him out of the country. Live to fight another day, like they said. Except that Richter had had a bait of fighting. He was in the mood for a long spell of peace and quiet. He would even settle for Kopec's mud cantina and rotgut tequila. But the first thing he had to do was to make it back across the Bravo . . .

He couldn't do it.

Udall had known all along that he couldn't, but Richter was just learning it for himself. There was only one place he had to make for, and that was Glory.

He didn't let himself wonder why. There didn't seem a chance of reaching Glory before sunup—and by that time Cabot would probably be dead and buried deep in a coyote-proof grave. So it wasn't the notion of saving the Ranger's hide that drove him toward the basin. Nor was it any thought of clearing himself of Udall's trumped-up murder charges—he would have needed Cabot's help for that.

It might have been a sense of pride that drove him. But a year of Kopec's tequila hadn't left him much of that. It could have been anger. He *did* still have some anger left. The only other reason was Jessie Marchand—and it didn't seem likely that he would risk everything, including his life, on account of a cantina girl.

Still, there it was.

He made himself think about getting over that towering hogback hump to Glory. There was only one way to do it; along the wagon track and through the pass. And Udall's men would be watching the pass.

Well, that couldn't be helped.

He began making his way up the rocky incline, every step of the way cursing Cabot for taking the Thoroughbred. Not to mention the guns. He climbed steadily. Hating Cabot gave him something besides bruises and scratches and aching lungs to think about. Then he remembered that within an hour or so Cabot would probably be dead. Certainly Udall couldn't allow a Ranger to report his suspicions to the authorities in El Paso.

Richter paused, clinging to a jagged outcrop, to get his breath. His legs quivered, his lungs burned; the bout of fever had drained his strength. Anyhow, he thought, climbin' mountains is a job for goats, not horsemen. At this rate it would take him until sunup to reach the pass—that would mean laying low until dark again. By that time Cabot and Jessie Marchand both could be dead.

Once he almost blundered into a Udall posse. He dropped as though shot on the green spikes of Spanish bayonet, and the search party—six of them—continued on to the west along the wagon road. Maybe an hour later another party of six passed below him, along the foot of mountain wall, inspecting gullies and thickets and other likely hiding places as they went. The lead riders carried pitch-pine torches, lighting the area a garish red. Richter could smell the resonant black smoke. It was all like an ugly dream, or something seen through the distortions of fever or bad tequila. Like the cockfights that he had seen at Mama Sam's.

But this group, like the first one, went its way without seeing him. Sixteen men in all, counting the Udalls, beating the night brush. Richter did not find the odds very comforting.

But there was little sense in dwelling on something that he could do nothing about. He started again toward that dark gap in the knife-edge ridge.

He had no notion how much of the night was gone and how much was left. A sullen cover of stringy clouds covered most of the sky. Richter dropped and lay on his back, gasping for breath.

He couldn't get up. He had gone as far as he could, the shape he was in. Anyhow, he reasoned—as soon as he was capable of reasoning—what could he do, even if he did reach the pass? How could you deal with Udall guards, without a gun?

His thoughts drifted. Too bad about the Ranger. Just when Richter started to like somebody it seemed that something always happened to him. Maybe he was a born hoodoo.

He thought about the girl. Half a year with Pepe Groz and his bandits. That must be something for her to think about late at nights. It seemed that she deserved something better than a back table in a Udall saloon. Or a place like Kopec's. For want of something better to do, Richter tried to remember what she looked like. But her features came out blurred. Very distinctly he could recall the taste of liver hash, and pulque. And he could hear her voice, now brassy and brittle as glass, now gentle, soothing. But he couldn't picture her face. Maybe it was because he had never really looked at her in a way that counted.

He lay in needle grass and gravel, looking up at the black sky. One thing he could not escape. Jessie Marchand had given up a miserable life in Prosperidad for one both miserable and dangerous in Glory.

All right, he told himself wearily, move. He rolled over. He stood up on rubbery legs. He found the gap where the wagon road began falling away toward Glory. He fixed the point with a bleary eye.

He walked. And sometimes he crawled. And now and then he crept on all fours like a prairie lobo approaching a bunch of early calves. And finally he made it to the road. Then to the pass. He even made it through the pass before he dropped behind a twisted tower of sandstone and gave his whole attention to the business of breathing.

This consumed a great deal of time. Long rents had appeared in the cover of clouds. He judged, from the position of moon and stars, that daylight was less than two hours away. Far below his hiding place and several miles to the east he saw a few flickering lights. That would be Glory. An aroused and excited place it must be, Richter reasoned, to be showing lights this time of night.

He rolled over and gazed back at the almost perpendicular mountain wall. And for a moment the dark shape of a horseman silhouetted himself against the sky. A Udall guardian of the pass.

"Cleet . . . is that you?"

The words rolled softly down the slope, and Richter realized that the question had been asked before, two or three times, perhaps. In his exhausted state his brain had failed to make a note of it. From far to Richter's right a bored voice answered.

"What is it now?"

"I thought I seen somethin', down by the gap."

"What you seen was shadows," the bored Cleet said. "The last thing that Richter's goin' to do is get hisself trapped in this basin."

"I don't know," the first guard said doubtfully. "I'll have a look. You keep an eye on the ridge."

"Look all you want to," Cleet said, swallowing a yawn. "You won't find nothin'. I wish he *would* show up here; I could use the bounty money. But he won't."

"Just keep an eye on the ridge."

"Sure, sure," the bored guardsman said. "I never hired out to be no nighthawk—I aim to remind Udall of that when I see him."

The horseman near the crest of the ridge disappeared. Richter could see nothing. After a while he could hear the horse making its way down the side of the mountain wall.

The one called Cleet was elaborately uninterested in the whole affair. Once the cautious guardsman called, "Stay alive, Cleet. If the Udalls catch you asleep on the job . . ."

Cleet only grunted.

Richter studied the sky. Was it growing lighter in the east, or was it his imagination? The guard's horse kicked a loose stone and it clattered and banged like a runaway wagon and finally smashed against a large boulder near the V of the gunsight pass. Face it, Richter thought bleakly, that guard's got a curious nature. He won't never be happy until he satisfies hisself that nobody slipped through his pass while he wasn't lookin'.

Richter crawled in a small circle. He found a rock about the size of his fist. That would have to do. The guard was descending carefully, taking his time. Richter looked again at the clearing sky. No doubt about it, it was getting lighter. He sat with his back against the outcrop and waited with unaccustomed patience for the cautious guardsman to come to him.

Now Richter could see the gray, ragged walls of the pass. After a while he could see an indistinct mass moving slowly down the wall of rock. The guard's horse. But the saddle was empty. The rider, ever cautious, had dismounted and was leading.

That's good, Richter thought. I'll only have one hand to worry about; the other one will be holding to the bridle reins.

Richter got to his knees. Then to his feet. He pressed back against the outcrop. Slowly, the guardsman took shape in the murkiness of early dawn. He was a wide, heavyset bull of a man, reins in one hand, revolver in the other. He advanced cautiously along the road in Richter's direction.

If I stay right still, Richter told himself, and don't move, maybe he won't find me.

He would find him. A man as cautious as this one wouldn't let a suspicion go until he had checked it out thoroughly. From around the edge of the outcrop, Richter watched him come. He looked big and strong and grimly serious about what he was doing. There was nothing about him to give Richter any comfort.

The guardsman stopped in the middle of the road, his chin raised, sniffing the air like an old battle-experienced coyote. He sensed a strangeness, something that wasn't just right. He called quietly, "Cleet."

Cleet, more than a hundred yards to Richter's right, waited until he was called a second time before answering. "What is it now?"

"Come here."

"What for?"

"Come here." This time it was a command and no mistake about it. Richter heard Cleet grumbling. But he was coming toward them, afoot and blundering noisily among the rocks.

Fine, Richter thought bitterly. Another gun to deal with.

His chances against the first guardsman were slim enough. His chances against *two* Udall gunhands would be reduced to nothing at all.

There was no decision to struggle with, on Richter's part. The decision was ready made. He had to settle things with the bull-like guardsman here and now, before Cleet came on the scene.

But that cautious gunhand had grown more cautious than ever. He was standing there in the middle of the wagon road and wouldn't budge until his sidekick arrived to cover him.

On the far side of the outcrop Richter felt along the ground and scooped up a few bits of gravel. He flipped some of it against the far wall of the pass.

The man's head snapped around in that direction. Richter thought: *Now.* He jumped.

His rubbery legs almost failed him. He stumbled, reeled, almost went to his knees. It turned out to be the difference between living and dying. A wildly stumbling man does not make an especially good target. The gunhand wheeled suddenly, still holding fast to the bridle reins. The animal, startled, reared, jerking the guardsman off balance. Richter was almost close enough to be burned by the muzzle flash, but the bullet missed him. The gunhand's .45 was almost in Richter's face. The roar was earsplitting, numbing. Richter swung blindly with the rock, not at the man's head, as he had intended, but at the gun.

The noise of that revolver frightened Richter more than the bullet. As things stood, it was man against man. Or, counting Cleet, one against two, at the very worst. But the sound of shooting could bring a Udall army down on him.

He swung again at the hand that held the .45. The guardsman snarled in pain and rage, and the weapon clattered to the ground.

Richter and the guardsman dived for it at the same instant. Richter felt the rough stag handle with his fingers. He clawed at it with both hands as the heavier, more powerful man bore him down. Then a second explosion. Not nearly so loud as the first, for the muzzle was pressed hard in the guardsman's midsection.

A voice from the rocks above the pass was

calling excitedly, "Max! Max! What is it!"

Max wasn't speaking. Max had a small hole just below his breastbone, where the bullet went in, and a terrible, gaping hole in his back, where it had come out. He had died instantly, and the deadweight was unbelievably heavy on Richter's chest.

The guardsman's frightened horse had bolted and was racing in the harsh gray dawn toward Glory. Cleet was still shouting, "Max, what is it!" Richter managed to roll Max's body off his chest. Clutching the revolver, he scrambled back to his outcrop.

Cleet, it turned out, was young and reckless, as well as easily bored. Richter saw him leaping and jumping among the rocks and boulders, rushing headlong toward the sound of battle. "Max!" Then he saw the body in the road. In his astonishment he stood straight up in that hard, early-morning light. Richter started to call to him, to warn him to drop his gun.

But it appeared that Cleet was, among other things, not very bright. Or maybe he was only green and inexperienced. Still staring at his dead partner, he started down the side of the wall like a sleepwalker. Richter let him come. Until he reached the road.

Then he said, "That'll do, boy. Stand where you are. Drop the pistol."

The youth obeyed without even looking toward

the outcrop. He couldn't seem to pull his gaze away from the dead man.

Richter stepped into the clear as soon as Cleet's .45 hit the ground. This second guardian of Udall's pass was a big, pink-cheeked, slightly plump youth not long out of his teens. Richter had no wish to kill him. But that would be up to Cleet.

Richter gestured with Max's .45. "Move over here."

The boy moved. Richter quickly scooped up his revolver.

"There any more Udall men around here?" Richter asked.

Cleet shook his head.

"Just the two of you pullin' night guard? Wasn't there somebody supposed to spell you?"

"Who's to spell us?" At last he managed to turn his eyes from the dead man. "Ever'body's out lookin' for you and . . ." Nervously, he drew the back of his hand across his mouth. "You *are* Richter, ain't you?"

Richter squinted. "Lookin' for me and who else? You was about to say."

The youth shrugged. "The lawman." He glanced back at the body, half-smiling. "Funny thing about old Max. You never seen a more careful galoot. 'Stay alive,' he always said. 'Don't let nothin' get past you.' Look at him now."

"What lawman?" Richter asked.

"The Ranger. Can't nobody figger how he got loose. But he did. The Udalls is fit to be tied."

Richter stared. How Cabot had managed to slip free of the Udalls, he couldn't imagine. But he could think of no reason why Cleet should lie about it. It explained why Udall had started night-time searches instead of waiting for daylight.

Cleet looked at Richter and shook his head sorrowfully. "Me and Max had it worked out to divide the bounty between us, if we was to catch you. A thousand dollars old Udall put up. Boy howdy," he said wonderingly, "what a fandango I could of throwed in El Paso!"

Richter looked at the young gunhand. No more than twenty-one at the outside. The chances were almost perfect that someone would kill him before he was twenty-two. Richter turned his thoughts back to Cabot and tried to decide if the Ranger's escape materially changed things as far as he was concerned.

Then, gradually, they began to hear the horses coming toward them at full gallop. His first fears were being realized. The shot had been heard by Udall's bounty hunters.

"Give a hand," he said to Cleet. Between the two of them they dragged Max's dead weight out of the road and dumped it behind the sandstone boulder. "All right," Richter panted. The horses were getting closer. "Listen to me, boy. I ain't got the time right now to learn you a proper set of manners—so just do like I say and don't ask questions. It might just be that you'll live to see tomorrow."

"Sure," Cleet said nervously.

"Get up there on the rocks, near the pass, where you can see what's goin' on. How good are you at lyin'?"

Cleet swallowed. "Good enough, I expect."

"I hope," Richter told him. "What you have to do is convince that bunch of scalp hunters that everything's dandy." He ran his fingers along the barrel of the gunhand's rifle. "If it turns out you can't convince them, I guess I'll have to kill you."

The youth licked his dry lips and nodded. Quickly, Richter ejected the cartridges in the rifle's magazine, took Cleet's cartridge belt, and handed him the empty weapon. "Up on the rocks."

With one nervous backward glance, Cleet mounted the rock wall. Suddenly Richter remembered Max's loose saddle animal. How was Cleet going to explain that horse?

He made himself settle down. Cleet would think of something. Somehow, he had almost unlimited faith in the boy's talent for lying.

"What can you see?" he called as soon as Cleet had reached the top of the wall that overlooked the pass.

Cleet shaded his eyes. "Six horsebackers. Mex vaqueros, looks like . . . Oh, oh." He shot a look down at Richter. "One of 'em's leadin' Max's horse."

Richter felt his stomach sinking. He tried to think of a reasonable explanation for a loose horse, not to mention a missing guardsman. He couldn't think of any. "Here they come," Cleet called. "I better make out I'm stickin' to business."

From his position beside the dead Max, Richter gazed at Cleet over the sights of his revolver. From here on out his life swung on a fragile string—it was all up to Cleet.

The horsebackers had eased their gait as they neared the pass. Richter risked a cautious look around the edge of the boulder. Six Mex cowhands, all heavily armed and hungry looking. They could almost taste that thousand-dollar bounty.

Cleet waved carelessly with his rifle and called a greeting in Mex. One of the vaqueros advanced ahead of the others and gestured toward the naked wall on the other side of the gap. "Udall says two guards up here. Where's the other one?"

Cleet laughed. "Where you reckon? Out lookin' for his horse. The one you caught, looks like."

Richter's instinct about Cleet had been a good one. He was a gifted liar.

The vaquero rode in a little closer. "Which way'd he go, this guard with the loose horse?"

"Down there somewheres." Cleet gestured vaguely. Suddenly he grinned, a thoroughly happy, disarming expression. "I reckon old Max'd be much obliged to you boys if you never said anything about this to the Udalls."

The Mex returned the grin, but faintly. "There was some shooting . . ."

Cleet didn't bat an eye. "What do you reckon scared the animal off in the first place? Snake. Like a damn fool, Max took a shot at it."

Actually there had been two shots, but Max, with the muzzle of the revolver in his gut, had effectively muffled the second one. Cleet lounged carelessly against the face of the rock wall. "Tell your boy," he said to the lead vaquero, "to tie a rock to the bridle reins. The horse'll stand quiet now till Max gets back."

The Mex seemed to sense that something did not smell exactly right. But a common vaquero was not in the habit of questioning the word of a gunhand. One of the riders got down, found a good-sized rock and tied it to the trailing reins. Slowly, and a little reluctantly, the vaqueros turned away.

"If you boys see that pard of mine," Cleet laughed, "tell him he can come back now. His saddle's come home again."

Richter breathed easier. But his mouth was dry,

and his hand shook slightly as he lowered the revolver. "Where they headed?" he called.

The gunhand shrugged. "Scoutin' the foot of the wall. Lookin' to see if you got in the basin another way, I guess." After a few minutes he said, "They're out of sight now." He started the climb back down. When he reached road-level he looked down at his dead partner and shook his head philosophically. "There never was a doubt in Max's head that he wouldn't die in bed someday." He grinned at Richter. "Mister, you've been a mean disappointment to Max. And me, too, for that matter. Old Udall ain't much partial to hands that make mistakes—and I guess he'd figger this a mistake, all right. Me and Max. Him gettin' his fool self killed, and me lettin' you through the pass this way . . ." He shrugged and started back up the wall.

"Where you think you're goin'?"

"To get my horse and put this place in back of me. I don't aim to get myself stuck through with old Udall's walkin' stick."

"Come back here," Richter said. But thoughtfully, not as a command. Cleet turned, scowling. "Maybe I can make you a better proposition," Richter told him.

The gunhand laughed bitterly.

"How much trouble are you in out there?" Richter gestured toward the other side of the basin.

Cleet shot him a slitted glance. Richter added, "I mean, drawin' gun pay from Udall. That kind of job's for them that can't get any other kind."

Cleet snorted. "Any fool can punch cows."

Richter shrugged. "How far can you get on the outside, without somebody like Udall to protect you, and without an old hand like Max to pard with? Two, three days I give you. Before some sheriff's deputy grabs you. Or maybe a Ranger."

He turned and tramped down the wagon road to where Max's horse was standing. There was a good Winchester in the saddle boot and an extra box of shells in the pocket. Richter felt a little better. A man with a good rifle under his knee didn't feel so helpless.

Still—he looked down at that flat, naked country that lay between the pass and Glory. Getting across that empty stretch in broad daylight would not be a simple proposition. He looked back over his shoulder and was not surprised to see Cleet, leading his own saddle animal, coming toward him.

"What you'd like to do," Cleet said thoughtfully, "is get down there to Glory without one of Udall's boys shootin' you out of the saddle. Ain't that right?"

Richter nodded.

"It might be," the youth said, "I could get you to Glory in one piece . . ."

213

"And turn me in for the scalp money?"

Cleet grinned sadly. "After what's happened here at the pass, I never would see that money. All I'd see would be the bottom of a grave—if Drago and his sidekick didn't throw me to the coyotes." He hesitated. "You in any way to strike a bargain with that Ranger, if we was to find him?"

Richter began to understand. Cleet had boxed himself in. On one hand he couldn't go on working for Udall, and on the other hand he was afraid of facing the law on the outside. But if he had a Ranger working for him, it would be a different story.

Richter had very little confidence in his ability to sway a Texas Ranger in pursuit of his duties, but he said, "How much trouble you in?"

"Maybe a holdup—just a rawhide saloon, not far from Laredo. And a few cows that got theirselves swum across the Bravo."

"What else?" Richter asked dryly.

"Nothin'. Well, there might of been another bunch of cows up north, in the Chickasaw Nation."

Richter sighed. "You never killed anybody?"

"Mister, old Max took me in and learned me to shoot. But I never killed nobody in my life—you got my word on it."

Cleet's word, Richter judged, would be about as much as Udall's pasteboard money. But somehow he believed him. Because of his youth, if for no other reason.

"If you're tellin' the truth," Richter said, looking down at the gravelly floor of the basin, "and if we can keep the Ranger alive long enough to listen, I'll see what I can do."

This was not at all what the gunhand had had in mind. But Richter had laid it out coldly, almost indifferently, on a take it or leave it basis. Cleet shrugged philosophically. He took it.

Chapter Ten

Cabot lay in the bottom of a dry wash staring angrily up at the morning sky. His leg was broken. His borrowed saddle animal was dead of a broken neck a short distance away. For what must have been several hours he had been cursing quietly and monotonously. There didn't seem to be anything else that he could do.

Who would have thought there would be cut banks on the flat, sheltered floor of a basin! He had always thought of cut banks as a plague of the prairies. He hadn't counted on these eroded gullies caused by water rushing down sheer mountain walls. He knew about them now.

He tried to comfort himself with the thought that things might have been worse. The dead horse, with Udall's brand clearly visible on its left hip, lay inches away from Cabot's twisted leg. At least the animal hadn't fallen on him. That, he supposed, was something. Also, the horse had been killed outright with the broken neck, which had saved it a good deal of pain. What if a leg had been broken instead of the neck? Would Cabot have dared risk a revolver shot to put the animal out of its misery?

It was a possibility that he preferred to leave unexplored.

Also, he told himself, he could just as easily have broken his own neck, or his back, or broken his skull instead of a relatively unimportant leg bone. He was alive. And that was something that he probably couldn't have bragged about if Emily Udall had left him tied up in that storeroom. He had an unpleasant feeling that the storeroom might have burned down before that night had ended. So simply being alive was not to be passed over lightly.

But the fact of being alive failed to cheer him. Sooner or later Udall's men were sure to find him. During the night groups of scalp hunters had passed within yards of the dry wash. And his leg was no longer comfortably numb. It was a brightly burning torch slightly below boottop.

So he comforted himself as well as he could with cursing. The most heartfelt passages he reserved for Richter, who had got him into this fix. He knew now that Richter had not killed Bob Venture, but that didn't help.

When he wasn't damning Richter's existence, he wondered about the Udalls in general and Emily Udall in particular. Cabot did not pretend to understand women. But Emily Udall, for sheer perversity, seemed to be in a class by herself.

It had been more than comfortably clear to Cabot that the girl had hated and feared him on sight. Yet, she had prevented Richter's old pal Tinkle, from quietly murdering him. And she had deliberately gone against her father and brother by turning the Ranger free. She had even returned his guns and given him a horse to ride. None of it made any sense. The bare facts, like loose parts of a puzzle, rattled irritatingly in Cabot's head.

Time dragged. A winter sun mounted slowly into a glassy sky. A breeze rustled the dry grass. Somewhere a lone horsebacker was cautiously crossing the floor of the basin. Cabot watched a large turkey buzzard hanging in the thin air high above the wash.

The horsebacker veered to the south, heading generally east, then tacked back to the north. He seemed to be getting closer to the wash. Cabot reached for his revolver.

It was midday and there were several customers in the saloon. A party of Udall bounty hunters had just returned for something to eat and a little rest before going out again. They were vaqueros, talking excitedly as they gulped fiery chili and beans and drank the sour beer. In Jessie Marchand they had an attentive listener.

The man known as Cabot had somehow escaped during the night. No one seemed to know how. But now there was a price on his head, the same as the one called Richter.

There were four of the vaqueros. Jessie Marchand moved to their table and joked with them in the little Spanish that she had picked up in Kopec's place, and in the mountains with the Pepe Groz bunch. The language she knew was a crude mixture of Spanish and Indian and not for polite society. The vaqueros were vastly entertained to hear such language from the mouth of a gringo cantina girl.

"The one called Cabot," she said, arrogantly drinking a vaquero's beer. "How'd he manage to escape the Udalls?"

The Mex cowhands shrugged elaborately.

"What did he do to get hisself on the Udall scalp list?"

The men grinned blankly and shook their heads. They did not talk about the men who employed them. They did not even think about them if they could help it. They did as they were told. It was the best way.

"What about the one called Richter? Has anybody collected the bounty yet?"

They shook their heads again, their expressions growing blanker. These questions made them nervous. If Jessie Marchand had learned anything in the past year it was that a good cantina girl was a good listener. She was quick to laugh, she drank whatever was set in front of her, and she didn't ask questions.

But a change had come over Glory since she had first landed here on an El Paso supplier's wagon. At first she had sensed an air of good-natured excitement. The vaqueros acted as though they didn't actually believe that the man Richter existed. They suspected that he was an *espectro* in their employer's head, and they treated the bounty offer lightly.

Now it was no joking matter. The *espectro* was real, and so was the bounty. Pedro, the Mexican gunslinger who palled with Drago, knew all about it.

The vaqueros bought Jessie Marchand a beer, but her strange dialect no longer amused them. They mopped their plates clean with limp tortillas. Then they stood and bowed with peasant politeness, and they left the saloon.

Jessie Marchand made herself sit at the empty table, in the empty saloon. Cabot had been found out. But he had somehow escaped the Udalls. She could not believe that he had escaped the basin. This was Udall's sanctuary or prison, whatever he chose to make it. At the same time, she had no doubt that Richter would find a way of getting *into* the basin when he began to grow impatient about the Ranger. Which wouldn't take long, if she knew anything about Richter.

The big blacksmith, one of the few men in Glory who hadn't gone scalp hunting, entered the saloon and asked for his usual noontime meal of chili and beans and tortillas.

Impatience mixed with anxiety made Jessie Marchand's skin prickle. She made no effort to understand her feeling for Richter. She treated it as a sickness that would one day go away, if it didn't kill her first. In the meantime she accepted it. In the beginning she had tried to reason with the thing; she had told herself that a man like Richter could mean only one thing—trouble. She had told herself that he was incapable of feeling anything but the emotion that drove him—hatred. He couldn't even feel contempt for a girl who had spent a year in the mountains with Pepe Groz.

The giant of a blacksmith had turned from the bar and was looking at her in a curious way. His name, Jessie had learned, was Larrs Mackison. She knew him as a silent, sour man, who did his work and lived as isolated as possible from the rest of the town. He obviously hated Glory, and probably the whole world as well. The only time Jessie had ever heard him speak was when he asked the Mexican bar woman for food. For this reason she was surprised when Mackison picked up his plate and beer and came to her table.

He stood towering over her, looking down at her with intense eyes. Clad as always in a heavy leather apron and a stocking cap, he reminded Jessie Marchand of an old Aztec god with a grimy face. He set the plate and beer on the table and took a chair. He ate steadily for perhaps three minutes and then pushed aside the empty plate. "You want a beer?"

She eyed him nervously. "All right."

He called to the bar woman. She brought the beer, collected the pasteboard and returned to her stove. "You don't remember me," he said.

Jessie shook her head. The prickle of uneasiness crept across her scalp. This had been the danger of coming to Glory in the first place. There was always the chance that someone would recognize her. Cantina girls, as a rule, were cut pretty much to the same pattern—but a Texas woman in a place like Kopec's would be remembered.

"No reason why you should," he said, with a bleakness of tone that was difficult to classify. "I was just a blacksmith then, like now. When Max Marchand's boy brought you to Sorano."

Jessie Marchand sat very still. "Your home in Sorano?"

He nodded. "Was, till I took it in my head to start my own wagon yard. Max Marchand already had a wagon yard—and you know Max. Never was a great one for competition; wasn't never happy without he was king of the hill." Mackison took a drink of beer and wiped his mouth. "One night my barn and stalls and sheds all burned down. I figured I didn't have much future there any more, so I pulled stakes . . ." He looked about him and laughed bitterly. "Looks like I got a knack for settin' up business in places where somebody wants to be king of the hill."

Burning out the competition sounded like her hidebound, Bible-quoting father-in-law. She

222

didn't blame Mackison for being bitter. But she didn't know what it had to do with her.

He said, "I remember what happened in Mexico. You and your husband. I was still in Sorano when old Max went after you. It ain't hard to figger in my mind the tone that red-necked old buzzard must of took. Might be you got to hate him nearly as much as I do."

"I finally got tired hating. I don't feel anything now."

The blacksmith didn't believe her, but he didn't mind if she didn't want to talk about it. "As you might of noticed, we got ourselves another Max Marchand right here in Glory."

Jessie hadn't thought of Udall as another Max Marchand. But Mackison had a point. She tasted the beer; it was warm and flat and she pushed it away. The last thing she wanted was to sit here hashing over old times with a hate-crazy blacksmith. But she sat quietly. There was something about this bitter giant . . .

"Tell you the truth," Mackison said with glittering eyes, "I never recognized you the first time I seen you. Two, three weeks ago."

She shot him an anxious, sidelong look. Two, three weeks ago she hadn't been in Glory.

He smiled, a half-sad expression laced with hatred. "I hadn't landed in Glory myself, at that time. Just driftin', you might say. On both sides of the Bravo. Well . . ." He spread his big hands on the table. "There was a Mex horse trader I knowed in a place called Prosperidad. I worked there a little spell, shoein' a bunch of Injun mules. Anyhow, that was where I seen you at. And the big horse-faced galoot called Richter."

Jessie Marchand took a deep breath and started to deny everything. But Larrs Mackison was quietly shaking his head. "I didn't make no mistake. You're Richter's woman. The thing that bothered me was what you was doin' here in Glory. Then we begin to hear about scalp money, and the man called Richter. . . ."

The blacksmith saw the gathering panic in her eyes. He spoke softly, and with surprising gentleness. "I been doin' some nosin' around. This place used to belong to Richter—him and some pals. Till Udall done them out of it." He leaned forward on the table, with that curious glitter in his eyes. "I know what it is to be done out of somethin'. By men like Udall. If your man's in trouble, might be I'm in a way to help." He stood up, and appeared to read her mind. "I'm not after the scalp money . . ." And after a significant pause, he added, ". . . ma'am."

A second horsebacker crossed the wash about a hundred yards below the place where Cabot lay. Now the basin spoke only in whispers . . . Quiet wind, and dry grass. Staring up at the spiraling buzzard, the Ranger began to lose himself in the vastness of the sky. He tried not to think of the pain in his leg.

The man landed in the wash with a thud, like a rock falling out of the sky. Cabot made a startled sound and grabbed for his revolver. But the young man with a steely smile held a .45 close to his head and said conversationally, "I wouldn't."

Before Cabot could make a decision about the revolver, there was a second thud and another man had fallen from nowhere into the wash.

The Ranger groaned. "Where the hell'd *you* come from?"

Richter grinned quietly, savagely. "Where you left me, afoot and with no guns, to deal with Udall's scalp hunters. We follered the buzzards, and here you was. Figgered somebody had to be alive here, or they would of landed." He scratched his jutting jaw. "How'd you get yourself in this kind of fix anyhow?"

The young man at Cabot's head yawned uninterestedly.

"This here," Richter said by way of introduction, "is Cleet. He knows this basin as good as I do, maybe better. He hired on with Udall as a gunhand. Did you know there was a bounty on your hide, same as mine?"

Cabot stared. He started to speak, but words failed him. Richter said, "Me and Cleet made kind of a bargain a while back. There's a thing or two against him—a holdup over by Laredo, and a case of rustlin'. I told him you'd be proud to knock these little things off his record if he'd pitch in and help us."

Cabot had grown a curious shade of purple. "Are you loco?"

Richter shrugged. "The thing is, I'm alive. And I might not of been if it hadn't been for Cleet. Tell you the truth, I wouldn't trust him no farther'n I could throw that dead horse of yours, but I'd rather deal with him than Udall."

Cleet grinned placidly. Cabot sputtered. "You know I don't have that kind of authority."

"Wasn't authority I was thinkin' about. You've got pals that maybe owe you a favor or two . . ."

"No," Cabot said coldly.

Richter shrugged. "All right, if you'd rather lay here till Udall's boys find you. Cleet knows all the Udall vaqueros; he can pass us off as new gunhands. For a little while. Unless we hit bad luck and run into somebody that knows us."

Cabot swallowed with great difficulty. "A rustlin'—maybe. A holdup—maybe. If there wasn't nobody shot."

Cleet spread his hands in grinning innocence.

"Now we've got that settled," Richter said, "maybe you better tell us how you come to be layin' here with a busted leg and a dead horse with a Udall brand on its hip."

Through gritted teeth Cabot told them what had happened. From the near disaster with Tinkle in the saloon, to the confrontation with Juan Gomez. Richter sighed. "Sorry day I ever run into Gold Tooth and that pard of his." Then Cabot told them about his next meeting with Tinkle, and his release by Emily Udall.

Richter was silent for several seconds. "Somethin' here I don't like," he said worriedly. "Emily Udall—I'd rather take up with a hydrophobia skunk. I can figger how she'd be skittish about killin' a Ranger, but it ain't like her to go against her brother and the old man."

Cabot's bluish lips twisted sardonically. "I figgered you'd show more curiosity about your pal Tinkle. Why'd he want so bad to see you dead?"

"That," Richter said softly, "is somethin' I aim to ask Tinkle when I see him." He gazed up at the dazzling sky. "What about the girl?" he asked at last.

"Jessie Marchand," Cabot said, with a note of irritation. "Can't you remember her name? She could get her hide nailed to a Udall door, because of you."

Richter flared. "It wasn't *me* that got her to leave Prosperidad."

But the Ranger had made his point, and he enjoyed Richter's discomfiture. Then he gestured wearily. "She's all right. Or was, the last I seen of her."

Richter and the young gunhand stood up. "That

227

leg'll have to be set and splinted before it starts to swell." Richter nodded to Cleet. "See what you can find. Straight sticks and a piece of piggin' string."

"There's not time for that!" Cabot snarled. "You spotted them buzzards; Udall's men are sure to do the same."

Silently, Richter began cutting off the boot. The Ranger's face was the color of tallow and beaded with sweat when Cleet returned with the sticks and twine. "Had to take the cord I tied my saddle roll with." He gazed good-naturedly at the Ranger. "Too bad we ain't got some whiskey. I've seen men holler like coyotes under a full moon when them busted bones rake together."

Richter had the boot cut away but he didn't touch the leg. "Tell you the truth," he said matter-of-factly, "I'd just as soon not have any hollerin' right now."

Cleet, standing behind the Ranger, caught Richter's eye and grinned. In the most casual way possible, he drew his .45 and cracked the barrel smartly across the side of Cabot's head.

From the top of the flatiron rock where they lay they could look down on the roofs of Udall buildings and sheds and, farther east, the town. The big house was still unfinished, Richter noted. Most of the smaller buildings were slap-up affairs of poles and rawhide, lending an air of

228

impermanence to the place, despite all of Udall's work. The town, the Udall homeplace, the whole basin, for that matter, looked deserted. "Quiet," Richter said uneasily.

"It won't be for long." Cleet pointed to a streamer of dust that was slowly rising in the north end of the basin.

Richter sighed. "I guess they found your pard."

Cleet grunted. "Somebody has. It would of suited me better if they'd waited a while . . ." He began backing down to the ground.

Richter looked at him suspiciously. "Where you think you're goin'?"

"To stop that horsebacker. My hide won't be worth a dobe peso if he gets word to Udall that Max's dead and I'm missin'."

Richter thought it over. It did make sense that Cleet's usefulness would be severely limited if Udall learned that he and Richter were in cahoots. "How you aim to stop him?"

Cleet grinned. "These Mex vaqueros'll believe anything."

The gunhand mounted and rode casually out to head off the messenger. Richter fumbled at his pocket for cigarrillos that had long since been used up. He didn't like the notion of teaming with a gunshark. But Cleet had been a big help with Cabot, stowing the Ranger in among the big rocks along the east wall. And they had come as far as they had, Richter realized, only because Cleet had scouted ahead, giving him plenty of warning when Udall bounty hunters appeared.

Richter turned his attention to the various buildings and corrals that were the Udall headquarters. Somehow he had avoided thinking too much about Tinkle. But now, for a few seconds, he let himself think about his old friend.

It left a hollowness in his gut. He had been right to avoid it. Still, it was interesting that Tinkle, of all people, should be the one to survive Udall's sweep of the basin.

The pistol shot was flat and uninteresting, little more than a pop, by the time the sound reached Richter's ears. He turned just in time to see the vaquero pitching out of his saddle. Cleet grabbed the loose animal's reins and went to work with a cool expertness that Richter had somehow not been prepared for. Quickly, the gunhand peeled the horse of saddle and bridle and set it free. He dumped the riding rig into a thornbush thicket. He made three tosses with his short lariat, finally caught onto one of the vaquero's big spur rowels, and dragged the body off by one leg. Like dragging a bawling calf to a branding fire.

Richter watched numbly as the killer indifferently deposited the body behind some rocks, shook his lariat free and rode calmly back to where Richter was waiting.

Richter said, with all the bitterness and contempt that was in him, "I thought you was goin' to give him a story!"

Cleet grinned and shrugged. "Shootin' seemed quicker and safer."

Chapter Eleven

From a comfortable saddle, the Udall headquarters had seemed reasonably near. Crawling through bunchgrass, and over gravel, through thornbush thickets and along gullies, it seemed considerably farther.

At the moment they were in a gully midway between the flatiron rock and the first line of corrals and headquarters sheds. Richter lay on his back panting. His shoulder ached but he was not particularly concerned with it. Clutching to dead Max's rifle, gazing up into that endless sky, his thoughts returned to Tinkle. A man who finished a war on the losing side did not come out with much. A few friends, if he was lucky. A strong sense of comradeship that often lasted as long as life itself. Richter had known that kind of comradeship once. But it had rotted and fallen to pieces. Richter had watched it happen and still could not entirely believe it. Hagle and Matthews—at least their end had come fast. But for himself and Tinkle—they marched to a slower dirge.

Cleet, peering over the lip of the gully, said, "You ready?"

"In a minute." He needed the rest. His muscles felt limp and spongy.

The gunhand built himself a smoke and lit it. "You don't reckon that Ranger pal of yours would be lyin', do you?"

"He'll do like he promised, if you told him the truth. If you haven't got a killin' against you."

"It's the truth." Suddenly he laughed. "Old Udall payin' me gun wage all this time. Here I am, never killed a man in my life."

"You got a mighty short memory. The man you shot out of the saddle a while back—the body ain't even cold yet."

Cleet scowled. "Hell, that was just a *Mex!*" He went back to scanning the stretch of gravel and grass that lay between them and headquarters. "Here's somethin'. One-horse rig comin' this way from Glory."

Richter took a quick look and groaned to himself. Cleet was saying in a puzzled tone, "The big ox drivin' is the blacksmith down at Glory. Some kinda bohunk, name of Mackison. The woman . . ." He glanced at Richter. "Somethin' funny here. Why would a crazy old blacksmith and a saloon woman be callin' on the Udalls?"

"Let's go," Richter said.

Cleet tramped on his smoke, and they eased out of the gully and continued the slow journey toward headquarters.

"Can't you go any faster!" Richter snapped at the gunhand.

Cleet, following a shallow depression that led generally toward the buildings, paused on his hands and knees and shot Richter a look of abstract interest. "A while back we wasn't in no hurry. Now we can't go fast enough. What changed your mind?"

"Just keep goin'," Richter snarled.

They kept going until the depression played out and there was nothing between them and the nearest shed but a flat stretch of gravel and shortgrass. They lay for a minute watching the buckboard circle some corrals and stop alongside the Udall house, the first Udall house, where they still lived. A Mex stablehand appeared from one of the sheds, loped toward the rig and then stood waiting to take the lines from the blacksmith. Another Mex, who was no stablehand, came toward them with a rifle.

"Well," Cleet said, "this here's as far as we go right now."

"We got to make it to the house."

Cleet shook his head. "Tonight, maybe. When it's dark. Not now." He nodded, indicating the Mex rifleman. "See that horsetooth gent with the rifle? That's Pedro. Wherever you see Pedro, another first-class gunhand ain't far behind. Name of Drago. It's their job to stick close to the family, and trail after an old pal of yours, I hear, by the name of Tinkle. See he don't get in any trouble."

Richter silently added up Cleet's bits of information. "That means Tinkle's someplace close-by," he said.

"Most likely. Or in the saloon at Glory."

"How do you know?"

The gunhand grinned. "They're the only places he ever gets to."

They studied the scene ahead of them. The big blacksmith sat on the spring seat like a rough-hewn piece of granite. Jessie Marchand seemed to be having an argument with Pedro. After a brief time another figure approached the buckboard from the far side of the house. Cleet grunted with satisfaction. "There's Drago. Now we know where everybody is."

"Everybody?"

"Well, Tinkle, anyhow, unless he's with the Udall men. And Miss Emily. The old man don't allow either one of them to ramble by theirselves."

Pedro and Jessie Marchand were still arguing. Now Drago got into it. Richter said, "You know Tinkle when you see him?"

"Everybody knows Tinkle. Before the Udalls come, he used to own this place."

Not quite all of it, Richter thought. "If some-thin' comes up," he said, "I mean, if things start to happen around here, Tinkle's to be let alone. No matter what happens, I want him kept safe and sound. You hear me?"

"Sure," the gunhand said indifferently. Richter wasn't fooling him with that "safe and sound" business. Richter wanted him kept safe and sound until he could gun him down himself. That was fine with Cleet.

"What's this?" Richter asked sharply. A figure had appeared at the back door of the Udall house. What must have been a loud argument between Jessie Marchand and the two gunhands stopped immediately. All heads turned toward the house when Emily Udall stepped out to the rear gallery.

Richter recognized her at once. Even from this distance of several hundred yards, there was something special about her. She stood quite erect there in the shade of the gallery, and suddenly everything was quiet and orderly. She could do that. And it was something more than simply being a Udall; it went deeper than that.

"There's a woman!" Cleet said admiringly. "Shame she ain't the kind that takes to gunhands."

Your future's chancy enough, Richter thought. You don't need the likes of Emily Udall to haze you into the slaughter chute.

To Richter's surprise, Jessie Marchand got up from the spring seat and started to climb over the front wheel. Drago—obviously on Emily Udall's command—jumped to hand the cantina girl to the ground.

Jessie Marchand, with a certain stiff dignity

of her own, marched quickly across the stretch of yard and onto the gallery. Then, as the men stared, both women disappeared into the house.

"I'll be damned," the young gunhand said in stunned wonder. "Did you see that!"

Richter had seen, but he did not entirely believe his eyes. Drago and his sidekick made for one of the sheds. The stablehand walked the blacksmith's horse to a barn, the blacksmith still sitting like rock on the spring seat.

"I don't like the look of this," Richter said.

"Wait till dark. We'll ease up to the house and nose around some." He looked at the sky. "Two, three hours, maybe."

Two or three hours. Nations had fallen in less time. But at the moment Richter could think of nothing better.

He wished he knew where Tinkle was. And he wished he knew what Jessie Marchand was up to. He felt in his pocket for the nonexistent black, rank cigarrillos that he had somehow become addicted to.

Eying him narrowly, Cleet produced makings. They silently built their smokes and lit them. "If we was smart," the gunhand said with little hope, "we'd crawdad out of here and get ourselves on the other side of the mountains. That Ranger must have some pals somewheres. You're goin' to need all the pals you can raise, if you figger to go up against . . ." Suddenly he snapped his smoke away and said in a tone of tired finality, "Look at this."

They spotted the wake of dust at almost the same instant. It rose in the rocks near the northwest wall and was now stringing out like smoke from a steam locomotive, on the basin floor. Richter counted seven of them, black moving dots in the distance. As the dots headed generally toward headquarters they became horsebackers. Long before he could see the faces of the men Richter recognized the two fine blooded horses in the lead, and that black, ridiculous hat of Henry Udall's. Siding the old man was the younger Udall, Giles. And behind Giles a lanky, string-bean figure that Richter knew only too well. He thought bleakly, now I don't have to wonder where Tinkle is.

Behind Tinkle and the Udalls were four vaqueros, their big hats tilted down over their eyes as they slanted into the lowering sun.

Richter looked sharply, now seeing that there were only three vaqueros. The fourth animal was more like a packhorse—but its burden was all too human in shape, arms and legs swinging stiffly to the rhythm of the march. *Cabot!* Richter thought in alarm. Somehow they had found the Ranger and had finished him off!

The young gunhand regarded the procession with a sardonic grin. "Well," he drawled, "they found Max, all right. Bet there was a loud to-do from old Udall when he found that pass unguarded."

Richter breathed easier. It wasn't Cabot's body they were bringing back, it was Cleet's dead sidekick.

Cleet scratched the fuzz on his jaw. "Surprises me some to see Tinkle ridin' with them."

They watched the riders pause for a moment on the rutted wagon track to Glory. Then the vaqueros, leading the fourth horse with the limp burden, headed toward the town; the two Udalls and Tinkle slanted toward headquarters.

"I'd be happier," Richter said grimly, "if Jessie Marchand got out of old Udall's house before he gets there."

Cleet frowned. "Jessie Marchand?"

"The . . ." He started to say cantina girl. "The woman with the blacksmith."

Half seriously, the gunhand said, "I never knowed saloon women had last names." He scanned the open spaces that surrounded them. "Tell you the truth, I don't much like this place we picked to lay out in."

Quite suddenly a dry, acrid smoke filled the depression in which they lay. "What the hell!" The gunhand stared about wildly. Behind them a small circle of red flame was eating greedily at the dry grass. Cleet and Richter jerked off their hats and beat the ground furiously. In a matter of seconds the fire was out. But the smoke lingered.

They fanned it with their hats, cutting it into small pieces, shredding it. At last the smoke too was gone.

They lay on their backs, breathing hard from the sudden exertion. "I'd be obliged," Richter said angrily, "if you wouldn't throw any more live smokes in dry grass."

His first instinctive fear had been the fear that any cowman holds for grass fire. Cleet had only been concerned that it would give their position away. He rolled over and scanned the area between himself and headquarters. "Nothin' to holler about. Nobody seen anything."

"Just the same . . ." But Richter let it drop.

Tinkle was tired and edgy and needed a drink badly. They had scoured the basin and found no sign of Richter or the Ranger. What they had found was a dead gunslinger at the pass, and a Udall saddle horse with a broken neck.

The Udalls rode a length ahead of Tinkle in grim silence. They had plenty at the moment to be grim about. Henry Udall had that "last ditch" look about him. Until recently he had taken all misfortune in stride. After all, he was a Udall, his son and daughter were Udalls. They were the Royal Family and this was their kingdom.

But they didn't know Richter as Tinkle knew him. Richter had hoped to salvage something from the war, and the partnership was all he'd had to work with. And when Richter got hold of a notion he clung to it like sandburs to a long-haired goat. Tinkle had told himself more than once, I ought to of killed him that day. Along with the marshal.

He sighed thirstily and gripped the saddlehorn to keep his hands from shaking. Too late now to worry over past mistakes. Udall's wolfish instincts had been right about Richter. Tinkle should have listened then, when it might have done some good.

Udall's original scheme had been foolproof, perfect. He had known for some time that Marshal Venture would have to be killed.

It had started with a mild case of bribery. Drago and Pedro and a few other gunhands had serious charges against them on the outside. In return for Udall cash, Marshal Venture had found it convenient not to recognize the out-laws whenever he happened to be in Glory. This arrangement worked well for everyone. The marshal settled all his debts and had money to spare. The gunhands could devote their attention to their jobs and not worry so much about juries and hanging ropes. It was an ideal arrangement. Everybody was happy. Then Venture had become greedy.

The deaths of Hagle and Matthews had intrigued the marshal. Deaths of violence, according to law, were to be reported to the county authorities who in turn would investigate and take appropriate action. Venture had assured the Udalls that the county sheriff would gladly take his word concerning the tragedy and not bother with an investigation.

What Venture did not mention right away was that he had visited the old Mex woman who had washed and laid out the bodies the day after the shooting. He was not surprised to discover that both of the fatal slugs were from rifle cartridges. Hagle and Matthews had been armed with revolvers only. Furthermore, Venture decided that the two recovered bullets would just about fit Pedro's old .44 rimfire Henry. When he was sure of his facts he went calling on the Udalls.

What Venture had in mind was a certain piece of grassland along the Palo Duro in the northern end of the Panhandle. He'd had a bait of marshaling. It would be pleasant to finish his days in peace, on a place of his own. Pleasant but expensive.

Udall heard him out with a straight face. "I see," he said. And that was when he knew that Venture had to be killed. "You understand that I can't produce that kind of money on a moment's notice."

Venture was relieved; he had expected a hot and unpleasant argument. "Take your time," he said generously. "Just so's I can move my wife in by calvin' time."

Udall assured him that everything would be settled long before spring. And so it was. For Marshal Venture.

A second double killing to cover up the first seemed to appeal to Udall. But this time the marshal, in pursuit of his duty, was to be overcome by his prisoner and murdered. Loyal, law-abiding Udall men, would then conveniently appear, attracted by the shooting, and kill the prisoner. The prisoner, of course, would be Richter. All of Udall's problems would be solved.

Or almost all.

Tinkle had proved himself a tougher nut to crack than the Udalls would have guessed in the beginning. In an El Paso bank vault there was locked away a certain legal document. In the event of his death the document was to be turned over to Richter—but only in the event of his death. If Richter was not to be found, the document would be passed into the hands of the nearest Ranger . . . It was all a bit elaborate and theatrical, but it was effective. At times during the past year Tinkle had been a sore trial to the Udalls; that bit of legal paper had kept him alive.

Shortly before Richter's arrest on a trumped-up murder charge, Tinkle made a call at headquarters. To Henry Udall he explained in detail about the document. With no small satisfaction he watched the homicidal fire flare and die in Udall's eyes.

"All right," Udall said in a choked voice, "how much do you want for it?"

No haggling. Whatever the price, he was ready to pay.

In those days Tinkle was thoroughly sober. He hadn't been drunk since the war. "It don't come cheap," he said.

"I never figured it would. Just tell me how much."

Tinkle smiled. Without that document he would be as good as dead. They would find him face-down in the gravel, the way they had found Hagle and Matthews. "It's not for sale."

Udall's expression did not change. He hadn't really expected Tinkle to exchange his one hold on life for dollars. "Then what is it you want?"

"Your daughter," Tinkle told him.

Thinking back on it, it seemed a curious thing that Henry Udall hadn't raved or cursed or run him through with that sword cane that was always with him. He did nothing. He didn't even look very surprised. "You're out of your head," he snapped. "Ask for something that I'm free to give."

"You gave her to Hagle, didn't you?"

In the days and weeks that followed the scene this is where it always ended, when Tinkle thought of it, which was often. He could not recall what Udall had done or said. He could not recall leaving the house and riding all the way across the basin to the place where he and Richter kept their camp.

He did, however, remember the way Richter had looked at him, with concern and worry. "Are you comin' down with somethin'?"

"No. I'm fine."

"You don't look fine. I've got some whiskey in my roll . . ."

"I told you I'm fine!" He realized that he was yelling at the top of his voice. After that, he would have given a year of his life for the whiskey in Richter's roll, but he couldn't bring himself to ask for it.

The next day a vaquero caught Tinkle in the north pasture and told him that Udall wanted to see him.

Twenty-four hours had changed Udall a great deal. For one thing he looked several years older. "I've been thinking over what we were talking about yesterday."

"Did you talk to your daughter?"

"No. And I won't." He raised his hand as Tinkle was about to speak. "Don't threaten me again. I understand what you are capable of. Yesterday you suggested that I . . . encouraged Emily to marry Hagle. That isn't true."

Tinkle laughed.

"It isn't true," Udall repeated. "At the time I'd never given it any thought. But this basin, cut off from most civilization, must have been a drab, lonesome place for a spirited girl. Well . . ." He found the speech heavy going. "Anyway, there was Hagle, always around headquarters. The only man around, you might say."

"Is this why you had me ride all the way from the north pasture?"

"I'm trying to explain how my daughter came to marry your friend Hagle."

"Is that all?"

Udall fumbled with his cane. "No. I thought maybe you'd like to leave that cowcamp and move up here to headquarters. That's as much as I can do, Tinkle. You can threaten me with hellfire or anything you like, but that's all I can do."

Tinkle thought it over. There was no turning back; he'd pulled his trail in after him. "I guess that'll do, for now."

"There is one condition," Udall said.

Tinkle's eyes narrowed.

"There is a little matter concerning our lawman friend, Marshal Venture. It's got to be settled. The sooner the better."

Udall had bluntly explained his plan for ridding themselves of Richter and the marshal with one stroke.

Tinkle had no feeling at all about the marshal. But kill Richter? That was something he was not prepared to do.

But Udall took his silence for agreement. "I

thought we'd see it the same way. With Richter out of the way, the sole and equal owners of the basin will be you and Emily. Have you thought about that?"

Many, many times, Tinkle wanted to say.

Regarding Udall's scheme to rid the world of a worthless saddle tramp and a crooked marshal, Tinkle had one suggestion. Tinkle volunteered to do the killing himself.

"Why?" Udall was surprised. "Drago can do it just as well."

"It's a personal matter," Tinkle said.

Udall thought he understood. He smiled faintly and waved his cane. "All right. If that's what you want."

All that was a thousand lifetimes ago.

But this was now, today, and Tinkle no longer cared much about anything. He knew now that he should have killed Richter instead of sending him into exile. There had been a stretch of several days, Tinkle recalled, when he had felt rather proud of himself for not putting a bullet in his friend's back when he'd had the chance.

Suddenly he laughed. Up ahead, Giles Udall turned in the saddle and glared disapproval. The Udalls naturally assumed that he was drunk, that he had somehow smuggled a whiskey bottle into his saddle pocket.

They reined up on the wagon road and Henry Udall sent his vaqueros to Glory with the body of the dead gunslinger. Tinkle took no interest in the proceedings. He ran his tongue along cracked lips. He felt burned out, like the inside of a charred oak keg.

Tinkle and the Udalls bore right toward headquarters. Giles Udall was saying, "Richter can't get out of this basin. Nor the Ranger. Some of the hands are sure to locate them before sundown."

Tinkle smiled to himself. Giles was young; he sometimes said foolish things.

Tinkle gazed blearily at that great expanse of basin floor. He had once regarded it with affection, as if it had been a woman. But that was long ago. Now he was interested only in the confused numbness to be found at the bottom of an endless number of liquor bottles, which the Udalls thoughtfully supplied.

At first, when he had heard that the Ranger had escaped and that Richter was probably hiding nearby, he had known a consuming fear. But it hadn't lasted. The Udalls would look out for him and protect him.

Tinkle heard himself laughing again. A dry, cackling sound, like the bitter laughter of an old woman. The Udalls had reined up and were staring at him with concern.

Henry Udall's voice dripped with cold contempt. "I see now that it was a mistake to take you away from your bottle."

Tinkle grinned. He felt lightheaded, and the

impulse for more laughter was almost uncontrollable. "Might be you're right," he said, bowing in the saddle, a burlesque of the Udall manner. "Your boys ain't never goin' to locate Richter until he wants to be located. I was with him at the Wilderness, when the whole world was on fire." He smiled. "While the Udalls was runnin' blockades and sellin' to both sides."

Faint color mounted in Henry Udall's face. He had gone to great pains and expense to gloss that period of war profiteering. He didn't relish having it called to mind by a common drunk. Without a word, he reined again toward headquarters. As a matter of habit, Giles and Tinkle followed.

There had been a time when Jessie Marchand could have faced Emily Udall without the slightest sense of inferiority—but not since that time in the mountains with Pepe Groz. She sat bolt upright in a surprisingly uncomfortable chair. The room itself was uncomfortable; it was too small, and too much heavy Udall furniture had been crowded into it, stored there until the new house could be completed. A Turkish carpet was on the plank floor, blood-red and gold and faded blue. On the walls there were pictures in dark oval frames, and there seemed to be a great number of small tables, and footstools, and lamps with colored glass bases. All the things that the Udalls had collected and stored here in the cramped rooms of the "old house" until the new house was finished.

The richness and weight of the room could be intimidating, and it made Jessie Marchand sharply aware of the difference between herself and Emily Udall.

Emily Udall looked as coldly beautiful as one of the many porcelain statuettes that crowded the tiny tables. She sat across from Jessie Marchand and looked at her with mild curiosity. "Now," she said suspiciously, "perhaps you can tell me, Mrs. Marchand, why you felt that you had to talk to me. What do you have to tell me about my husband?"

It had been the mention of Hagle that had got Jessie Marchand past the two gunhands and into the Udall house. Worriedly, the cantina girl moved a hand across her face. She had nothing to go on, except her instincts. And the knowledge that within the hostile walls of this basin Richter could not possibly stay alive for more than a few hours, the way things were going.

She licked her tongue along her lower lip. "The gunhands out there," she started, "told you who I am. A saloon woman, down at Glory. They didn't tell you I am a . . ." She paused and smiled thinly. No matter what word she used, it wouldn't sound quite clean. "I'm a friend of Richter's," she finished.

Emily Udall did not look surprised. "I see," she

said. "And Richter has come to you for help. And you, knowing there is a price on his head, will tell my father where to find him. In return for the full bounty, of course."

Jessie almost laughed. Emily's swift examination of her motives told her more about the Udalls than she could have learned in a dozen years of eavesdropping. "That's not why I'm here."

Emily Udall frowned. She didn't believe her, but she decided to hear her out.

Jessie Marchand said, "There was some trouble in Mexico. Richter was hurt and I took him in. That's when I first heard about this place— Glory."

"And the Udalls," Emily added.

"Yes. And the four soldiers that came out of the war together—Hagle, Matthews, Tinkle, and Richter." She watched Emily Udall's face. Did it change? Was the paleness real, or was it a trick of the dim lighting in the room? "There was a while," she went on, "when Richter was at my place, and there wasn't anything to do but talk. The Mexican police were after him, and a Ranger, and maybe some of your father's gunhands." She shrugged. "Anyhow, that's how I heard about all this. Beginning with the partnership, the four soldiers."

Emily Udall sat rigidly erect. "I still don't understand . . ."

"The thing is," Jessie Marchand said quietly, "I was sour on the world. But Richter showed me I wasn't the only one that had troubles. It was a big thing to him, that partnership. It was the only decent thing he had. Then somebody ruined it." She looked directly at Emily Udall. "Was it you?"

Small spots of color appeared on Emily Udall's cheeks. "If that's all . . ." she said coldly.

Jessie preferred not to hear the ring of dismissal. "While he was at it, Richter talked a good deal about Hagle, the one you married. The whole thing was clear as springwater to Richter. Your father saw this basin, wanted it, and set hisself to get hold of it, any way he could. It must have seemed like the simplest thing in the world, when the partners started to make calf eyes at Henry Udall's daughter. Marry into the partnership—that was the easiest and quickest way to get a toehold here. And a toehold was all a Udall ever needed."

Emily Udall came out of her chair, her eyes flashing. "I was a fool to let a saloon woman into my house!"

Jessie studied her coolly. "I thought from the beginnin' that Richter might have been wrong about you and his pal Hagle. It never entered his head that you might have loved him. Just like it never entered your father's head. Or your brother's." There was a sudden sadness in her eyes. "I don't know. If your father'd known, maybe he never would have had him killed."

Emily Udall looked as if she had suddenly found herself face to face with a madwoman.

Jessie Marchand looked at her. "Think back. Who was it that figured out ways to throw you with Matthews when your husband wasn't around?"

Emily Udall's face was so pale that it looked almost blue in that heavily curtained room.

Jessie stood slowly. "This basin," she said. "The town. Everything here bears the Udall brand now. It means a lot to your father—I guess it means about everything to him. And what Henry Udall has, he keeps. He'd even kill to keep it."

"Not my husband!"

"Think back," Jessie said again. "When did Henry Udall ever stop at killin'? He arranged for a cowhand to be killed so that a murder could be charged to Richter. Why couldn't he arrange for a double killin', gettin' rid of two of the partners with one shot, almost. That would leave Richter—but Henry Udall already had plans for Richter. And Tinkle—maybe he had plans for Tinkle, too."

The smooth beauty of Emily Udall's face was now dry and lifeless. "Lies!" she said, the word hissing. Her mind raced to other things, away from the subject at hand. Her eyes narrowed and became cunning. "A saloon woman. A 'friend' of Richter's, as you put it. What brought you to a place like Glory, if it wasn't the bounty?"

"Richter's got the notion that the answer to his problems is here in Glory. He even convinced the Ranger that it was somebody else, not him, that killed the marshal. The Ranger got me to come on ahead and start work in the saloon, on the chance that I might be able to help Richter." She smiled crookedly. "Not even a Ranger likes to go up against Henry Udall with just a prisoner's word to go on."

Emily fixed her with an intense stare. "If the Udalls are as deadly as you seem to think, didn't it occur to you that butting into Udall affairs might just get you killed?"

Jessie Marchand played the only ace she had. "If Richter had been Hagle, and you had been in my place, wouldn't you have come?"

She didn't have to speak. The answer was clearly etched in her face. In her own peculiar way—a way so peculiar that probably not even Hagle realized it completely—Emily Udall had loved her husband.

A stifling silence was disturbed by an excited rattling of the back door. "Miss Emily, it's your pa and Giles!" It was the gunhand, Drago. "They're comin' back from the gap!"

Jessie had hoped to have something settled before the return of Henry Udall. A saloon girl in his house, on top of everything else—there was no guessing how he would react to that.

"Miss Emily!"

Drago too was worried about what Henry Udall might do. Emily turned stiffly and left the room. Jessie heard her saying, "Where's the rest of the search party?"

"Broke off and made for Glory. Tinkle's with your pa and brother." Then the gunhand spoke again, with a chilly grin in his voice. "Pedro says the vaqueros was leadin' a horse with a dead man across the saddle. Maybe the hunt's over."

Jessie Marchand felt the strength go out of her legs. She sank back down to the chair.

Chapter Twelve

The sun appeared to have stopped dead in the western sky. Richter was edgy and impatient, but he knew better than to try to cross that open stretch in the face of two experienced gunmen.

Cleet lay on his back chewing a piece of dry grass. He had learned to take things as they came. He didn't like the notion of letting out his gun to a nobody like Richter—still, it was better than being brought in across a saddle, like Max.

"I don't guess I ever told you about Pedro," the young gunhand said conversationally. "That sidekick of Drago's?"

Richter grunted, his eyes following Tinkle and the Udalls up the long grade from Glory, his mind leapfrogging from one violent prospect to another.

"Pedro," Cleet continued, "when he was just a shaver, lived a spell with the Yaquis. Now, if that saloon woman, or the blacksmith, was to know somethin' about you . . . It wouldn't take Pedro long to get it."

Richter glanced at him sharply. "You talkin' about torture?"

Cleet shrugged. "Every man, they say, has got a thing in his head that makes him special. With

Pedro—well, he learned to like the Yaqui way of doin' things."

Richter took a deep breath. "We're not waitin' for dark. Soon's the Udalls—and my old pard—get up to the house, we'll make our play."

The gunhand was almost afraid to ask what kind of play that might be.

Slouching wearily, ungracefully in the saddle, Tinkle looked again at that great flat bed of gravel and brush and grass that had cost everybody so much—and the paying wasn't over with yet. He was sick of the Udalls and the basin and cattle, but most of all he was sick of himself. His foggy thoughts kept going back to the beginning, back to the four soldiers that had first stumbled onto this place. Usually he did not allow himself to think about that. But now he was tired. And he had been away from the bottle too long.

The four soldiers, fresh from a tour in a man-made Inferno, had somehow managed to retain something of their original selves. Hagle, the laughing, eternal optimist. Matthews, the romantic encased in the bluff shell of the regular army. Richter, a drifter looking for a place to take root but never really believing that he would find it.

And Tinkle himself . . . how had he fitted in? The quiet, schoolmasterish Tinkle, who once had actually considered teaching as a profession. Long ago, when he was young.

Now he felt that he had never in his life been young. The expectations of youth had long since been burnt out of him. Or rotted out. The man who had fought war with honor, and even valor, had survived to learn what it was to be a coward. He had murdered the marshal, Venture, from ambush. Probably he would have murdered the Ranger, if Emily Udall hadn't stopped him. He certainly intended to kill Richter, if that chance came to him.

Even now, after all that had happened, he could not rid himself of the feeling that everything would somehow work out if Richter was done away with.

It was all quite vague in Tinkle's whiskey-numbed brain, and the only thing that was clear and sharp and never changed was the fact that he wanted Emily Udall. The price didn't matter. He was aware that she could not bear to look at him or speak to him except with contempt. It didn't matter. He could be as determined as the Udalls. He had no doubt that sooner or later she would marry him. She had married Hagle, hadn't she, driving the first wedge that had shattered the partnership? With Richter out of the way, the legal consolidation of Udall and Tinkle water rights would be an obvious Udall move.

Tinkle smiled wearily and swayed in the

saddle. There was only one way for the Udalls to achieve that consolidation; another matrimonial wedge, the final wedge which would destroy the partnership completely, leaving Udall the lone owner of his self-chosen little kingdom.

After countless bottles of Udall whiskey, Tinkle's power to reason had been reduced to a kind of shapeless cunning, an animal instinct for survival in which the human will to survive had been omitted.

It had occurred to Tinkle that Udall gunmen might well have had a hand in the deaths of Hagle and Matthews. It seemed a fine distinction at this point, and thoroughly unimportant. If Hagle and Matthews hadn't actually killed each other, sooner or later they would have. Because that was the way the Udalls had planned it.

He did not doubt that they would think up some such end for himself when his use to them was over. He simply did not think about it.

There had been a certain gray morning in El Paso, in the street in front of the Del Norte, when he had looked on Emily Udall for the first time. Nothing else, since then, had really interested him. She had had her effect on all of them. With Hagle it had been instant, cow-eyed love. With Matthews it had been a ridiculous mixture of old world chivalry and dumb fascination. Richter, Tinkle recalled, had reacted differently from the others. He had cautiously kept his distance, and

Tinkle had detected traces of suspicion and even fear in Richter's manner whenever he was near her. Tinkle's own reaction had been violent and obsessive, though the others had not noticed.

It all passed through Tinkle's mind, ghostly figures moving in an alcoholic fog. He lurched in the saddle, and Giles Udall looked back at him, his thin mouth curled in disgust. Tinkle smiled to himself. Sir, he thought, there'll come a day, soon, when you will have to swallow your sneers. The day that Emily Udall becomes my wife.

The strange thing about it was that he did not love her. He feared her contempt, and sometimes he hated her. His first emotions had quickly sickened and died. All that was left was the compulsion to own her, to have her wear his brand. It would not make him a man but it might make him less of a nobody. To bring the Udalls to their knees, if only for a moment. That was the thing that drove him.

It was a shabby ambition, and he knew it. But that didn't matter either. At some point he had wandered onto a crooked road, and this is where it had led him.

They left their horses at the rack beside what was already known as the "old house." Henry Udall was tired, tireder than he could ever remember being before, but he consoled himself with the thought that it would soon be over. They had found the dead horse—the animal that Emily had so stupidly and uncharacteristically furnished the Ranger. So the Ranger was still in the basin, afoot and probably injured. Attending to Cabot would be a simple matter. It was the action of his own daughter that worried Henry Udall.

Never in her life had his daughter gone contrary to her father's wishes. That she had done so now disturbed him more than the knowledge of Cabot's escape or Richter's presence in the basin. He could not imagine how, but in some way he must have offended her, angered her.

Well, that could be remedied. He would make proper amends and then forgive her for her foolishness. And everything would be the same as before. The Udalls standing as one, powerful, unassailable, like these great rock walls of the basin itself.

The stablehand was loping toward them to take the horses. Drago and Pedro were also crossing the gravelly yard at a quickened gait. A big, unfamiliar figure stood by the side of one of the sheds, beside an unfamiliar buckboard. Henry Udall looked at his son. "Who's that man?"

Giles turned and looked. "Blacksmith," he said. "I gave him permission to work in Glory."

"Why?"

"You know how blacksmiths are. Bohunks, most of them, drifting here and there. The other blacksmith had pulled out, so I put this one on."

It was a reasonable explanation. Blacksmiths tended to be more independent than store-keepers. If they didn't like a place they simply packed their few tools and pulled out. But what was this one doing here at headquarters?

Drago and Pedro pulled up panting. "We seen the Mex hands headin' off toward Glory. Was that Richter they was leadin'?"

Henry Udall shook his head. "One of the guards at the pass. The second guard is missing too. Do you know who it was?"

Drago thought. "There was a young firebrain, name of Cleet. Him and Max was sidekicks."

"Well," Henry Udall sighed, "Cleet's missing. Probably struck for the outside when he saw that he might have to earn his gun pay. His friend we brought in across the saddle." He shrugged the matter aside. "Get us some fresh horses," he said to the stablehand. "We'll be riding out again in a few minutes. You, too," he added to the gunhands.

Resting against the hitchrack, Tinkle seemed half asleep. The Udalls ignored him. Henry Udall turned abruptly toward the house when Drago said uneasily, "There's somethin' I better tell you."

Udall looked around impatiently.

"The blacksmith brought somebody up from Glory."

Udall scowled. He was in no mood to receive visitors, even important ones.

Drago said, "Matter of fact, it was the woman from the saloon."

Henry Udall's expression was a blend of irritation and puzzlement. "What are you talking about?"

"The new saloon girl," Drago said unhappily.

A saloon girl in a Udall home! Henry Udall was not too tired for outrage. "A woman like that! Why didn't you send her packing?"

"Just what I aimed to do." Drago spread his hands helplessly. "But Miss Emily wouldn't have it."

The two Udalls stared at each other. Tinkle, his eyes almost closed, displayed only the faintest kind of interest. "Well," Henry Udall said stiffly, "I'll see about this. You and Pedro get the horses."

The Udall men stood for a moment in the doorway of the overcrowded, faintly musty room, glaring disapproval at the two women. Emily Udall smiled, but it was not an expression calculated to set her father's mind at rest. "Father," she said coolly, "this is Mrs. Marchand . . ."

Henry Udall glared at his daughter without acknowledging the existence of Jessie Marchand. "What is the meaning of this!"

Emily appeared to ponder the word. "Yes," she said slowly, her eyes icy and dark, "it's time we talked about the meaning of things."

Giles Udall started to speak, but his father cut

him off with a slashing gesture, as vicious as a saber cut. He no longer showed his exhaustion. He looked angered and hurt.

"We might start with the death of my husband," Emily said.

Jessie Marchand sat very still. Somewhere in the house a clock was ticking. It was the only sound to be heard.

Henry Udall stood rigid and bloodless. His mind, Jessie knew, would be racing, searching all the dark corners of his memory for an answer to what was happening here. When he finally spoke, Jessie was surprised that his voice was perfectly natural, without strain or undue concern.

"Your husband, as you well know, was killed by a madman, who in turn was himself killed by your husband." Suddenly Udall took a condescending, fatherly tone. "Obviously, you're not yourself today. I'm afraid you're coming down with something." He turned briskly to his son. "Tell one of the hands to go into Glory. I believe there's a stock of medicines at the general store . . ."

His daughter was shaking her head slowly from side to side. Spidery fear lines in Udall's face lengthened and multiplied. He had confidently been telling himself that the blunt coldness in his daughter's eyes and voice was nothing but typical Udall hardheadedness. Now he recognized it for what it was. What he saw was hate.

Richter was feeling along the band of his hat for a match. The young gunhand watched nervously. "Look here, I never bargained . . ."

"You wasn't in no position to bargain," Richter told him. He located a match. Then he held up a wet finger and pinpointed the drift of the breeze across the basin.

"What you're aimin' to do," Cleet complained bitterly, "is get the bunch of us cooked like a ox at a barbecue."

"Maybe." Beside Richter lay several hard twists of dry grass about the size and shape of Mexican cigars. "But I don't aim to wait till night."

Cleet was sorry that he had ever mentioned Pedro's past association with the Yaquis. Even so, he couldn't understand Richter's concern. "Look," he said, "maybe I overdid it about Pedro. Anyhow, old Udall wouldn't put up with no Yaqui di-dos."

"Wouldn't he?"

The gunhand exploded. "What's the difference! She's just a common-run saloon woman!"

With a curious, one-sided expression on his homely face, Richter looked at the gunhand. Then he hit him. With all the strength in his good arm, and with the fury that had been building inside him for the best part of a year. The blow caught Cleet full in the face and sent him sprawling. His mouth was suddenly bloody, his eyes glazed. He stared at Richter and rage almost overcame him. Instinctively, his hand went for his gun.

At the last instant he changed his mind. Richter watched him coldly but had not moved. Almost as if he were deliberately inviting Cleet to make his gun play.

When somebody else's life was at stake, the young gunhand had the instincts of a badger. When it was his own life, he was not carefree. Cleet rose slowly to his elbows. Reason told him that a saddle tramp like Richter would not stand a chance against a trained gunman. And Cleet was well trained—Max had seen to that. Still, a voice in his head urged caution.

"What the hell'd you do that for!" It was almost a whine.

Richter put the incident from his mind. His whole attention had gone back to the open space that lay between them and the Udall headquarters. "If Udall's learned anything at all as a rancher he'll know the worst thing that can happen to a cowman is a grass fire. Whatever he's up to, he'll drop it to fight a fire. And if he hadn't got the sense to do it, his hands have."

He struck a sulphur match and lit a twist of grass. Cleet wiped his bloody mouth and watched in dismay as Richter lobbed the burning twist into the dry grass. Immediately the hungry fire began its work. He lobbed two more twists and then hurriedly backed down into the shallow gully. For a moment he watched the orange and yellow fire jumping and spreading along the slope. That was that. It was done and could not be undone. With a little luck the breeze would guide the fire past headquarters to the east wall where it would die for lack of fuel. With a little more luck, in the confusion, he might be able to get Jessie Marchand out of the house and away from the Udalls.

That was as far as his thinking went. In some way it had become very important that the girl be saved. More important than proving his innocence or regaining the basin.

Cleet was cursing expertly and steadily as the black smoke began running along the gully. Richter glanced at the far wall where they had secured Cabot among the rocks. If I don't get hung on a charge of murder, he thought, I'll probably get it for startin' a grass fire. In cow country the two crimes were of the same order.

At Udall headquarters, the stablehand was the first to see the boiling smoke. Richter and Cleet heard him yelling. Through the curtain of smoke they glimpsed figures scurrying among the sheds. Pedro was yelling something in Mex to the laborers working on the new house. Richter paused as figures poured out of the house onto the rear gallery. First Giles Udall, then the old man. Finally the two women, Emily Udall and

Jessie Marchand. Richter breathed a little easier.

The big blacksmith stood wide-legged, hands on hips, near his buckboard. He stared at the spreading fire with the air of a vengeful god tasting satisfaction.

Richter and Cleet continued along the gully until it played out. A small cluster of Udall outbuildings stood between them and the fire. They stopped a moment to get their breath. "When he finds out who set that fire," Cleet said bitterly, "old Udall won't be satisfied just to shoot us. If he don't give us to Pedro, he'll carve us up in bite-size pieces with that damn walkin' stick of his."

Richter shot him a sour grin.

They began moving on headquarters behind a curtain of smoke. They scrambled through a pole corral and pulled up alongside a harness shed. There was a pistol shot. They moved on to another shed and saw that Pedro had shot a spotted calf that had been put up for slaughter. The laborers were running toward the fire with wet sacks and bits of tarpaulin, but Drago and Pedro worked calmly and quickly on the calf. They slit the animal with knives and laid it open. Pedro methodically divided it into two bloody halves with an ax.

Richter nodded grudging approval. They were making wet drags, and there was just a bare chance that they might stop the fire with them.

Pedro hurried off, then soon returned with two saddled horses. Each man fixed his lariat to one half of the animal and rode toward the blaze.

Halfway across the yard Henry Udall shouted something to his gunhands and pointed to the blacksmith. Apparently he was under the impression that Larrs Mackison had started the fire. Pedro reined up sharply, grinning at the blacksmith.

Richter felt himself go cold. Mackison was slow to understand the meaning of that grin. Pedro shot him with no more emotion than he had shot the calf a few minutes before. Shot him twice before anyone could move. Mackison sprawled in the dirt.

The women stared. But the incident had captured only a small part of Udall's attention. He shouted angrily to the laborers who had turned to see what was happening, and they returned quickly to their work.

A dense smoke lay over the headquarters buildings, a black awning that showered gritty black ash down on the figures below. Down in the town a group of citizens had gathered in the street to watch, but no one made any move to help. Four vaqueros came out of the saloon and raced for their horses; they were the only ones in the settlement to show any interest in saving the town, or the Udalls, or even the basin itself.

Drago and Pedro dragged their bloody halves

of the calf along the outer edges of the fire, but they only scattered flying sparks into more dry grass and started more fires. Some of Glory's citizens brought out wagons and teams and began loading their personal belongings. A handful of horsebackers had already started toward the pass.

Flying sparks had started a small fire near one of the sheds. The two Udalls hurriedly began beating at the flames, and even Tinkle roused himself to help. The two women did nothing. They were still staring at the dead blacksmith.

Richter took stock and decided that it was unlikely that the situation would become more favorable than it was now. He spoke over his shoulder to Cleet, "I'll try to get the Marchand woman over here. You think you can get her up to the rocks where the Ranger is?"

Cleet nodded unhappily. "But I don't know what good it'll do. Sooner or later Udall's boys'll find us."

He moved away from the shed and tried to get Jessie Marchand's attention. She didn't see him. He even yelled, but there was so much yelling that she didn't notice. At last he thumbed a loose .45 cartridge from his belt and heaved it at her feet.

Her eyes were large when she saw him. He gestured for her to move away quietly and meet him on the far side of the outbuildings. She nodded, indicating that she understood.

Suddenly Richter swore under his breath. He had meant for her to come alone, but she had taken Emily Udall's arm and was leading her away from the commotion, leading her quietly, as she might have led a dazed or fascinated child.

The Udall men and Tinkle were still busy with the shed fire. Everybody else, including the vaqueros from Glory, were fighting the fire on the slope.

Many times Richter had noted the way men were dazzled and blinded by Emily Udall's beauty, but he hardly saw her as the two women slid silently toward them through the rolling smoke. His gaze followed Jessie Marchand who somehow managed a look of pride despite her soot-streaked face and the gaudy rig that she wore in the saloons.

Cleet studied Emily Udall with hopeless admiration, and then shrugged resignedly and became bored by it all. The women reached the shed, gasping and coughing. Jessie Marchand stared at Richter.

Richter had the foolish notion that he wanted to touch her. But he didn't. "I don't know what brought you up here from Glory," he said coldly. "Don't you know that that sidekick of Gold Tooth's is on Udall's payroll now?"

She shook her head dumbly, unable to fit that small fact to the present situation. Richter said angrily, "Cabot was a fool to send you here in the first place. And you was a fool to come." With a jerk of his head he indicated the gunhand. "This here's Cleet, one of Udall's gunsharks. He decided to switch sides, but that don't mean you can trust him." He pointed toward the east wall. "Cabot's up there in the rocks with a busted leg. Cleet'll show you the way . . ."

He glanced at Emily Udall. The change in her face startled him. All their faces were blackened and glistening with sooty tears. But these were not smoke tears. She paid little attention to what they said or did. She reminded Richter of a beautiful but dirty faced doll that shed real tears.

Jessie Marchand said, "I think you can prove you're not guilty of those murders."

"Includin' the marshal?"

"Yes."

Richter hesitated. "How?"

She glanced at Emily Udall. "Tinkle told her about the marshal and how he arranged to have you charged with the murder. Also the murder of the vaquero. Also . . . her father arranged the murder of Hagle."

This was no surprise to Richter.

Then she added, with a touch of gall, "I guess it never entered your head—maybe it didn't even occur to Hagle—but she loved her husband."

Richter blinked several times and then said flatly, "You're loco."

"Look at her. After all this time she's finally

come to believe the truth about her husband's death."

It was an eerie, unreal scene, and all of them seemed to realize it at once. The sun had dropped behind the east wall and the sky was red. It seemed that all the world and even the sky was burning, and there they stood talking, talking. Talking nonsense.

He turned angrily to Cleet. "Get them out of here, both of them."

"What about you?" Jessie Marchand asked.

"There's somethin' else to be seen about." He glared at the gunhand. "Get started."

They had waited too long. Above the general uproar they heard Henry Udall shouting, "Emily, where are you?"

Emily heard the voice but did not answer right away. She looked at Richter, and in her eyes was the glittering cold of distant stars. "You knew about my husband? The way he died?"

Richter knew that he should be preparing to make a stand. "I had a notion. But it was nothin' I could prove."

"How was my husband killed?"

"Maybe him and Matthews shot each other, like the story has it. But most likely Udall gunsharks had a hand in it."

"You can't prove that."

Richter shook his head. *"No."*

"It may be," she said slowly, "that I can."

273

She moved away from the shed. It did not occur to the others to try to stop her. Perhaps because she was a Udall, and Udalls did as they pleased. They watched her melting in the swirling smoke which was now a ghostly, pink-tinted fog. Henry Udall called anxiously, "Emily, is that you?"

Richter gestured for Jessie Marchand to crouch low behind the shed. The young gunhand lay on his gut at one corner of the small shelter and stared watery-eyed over the sights of his revolver. Richter moved to the other side with the rifle and took a position behind an oak chopping block.

There were more pistol shots on the slope. The vaqueros were killing more cattle, or possibly horses, for wet drags. From where he lay Richter could not see much of the fire-fighting. He could, however, see the ghostly figures of Emily Udall and her father. Over to his right Giles Udall and Tinkle had given up on the burning shed. The roof had already fallen in and the walls were beginning to buckle.

"Tell me, Father," Emily Udall was saying, "how did my husband die?"

Richter could not see Henry Udall's face clearly, but it must have showed profound shock and hurt. The world was burning and the gods were dying, and his daughter plagued him with idiotic and pointless questions. His voice became slightly shrill in anger. "Emily, what in heaven's name is the matter with you!"

"I want to know," she insisted.

Udall groaned, then gained momentary control of his emotions. "He was a nobody," he said icily. "I don't understand you at all, Emily, for bothering me at a time like this! You knew all along—you must have known—the plans we had for Hagle, after the wedding."

"I didn't know you planned to kill him."

"We didn't exactly plan it. It just worked out that way."

"I loved him," Emily Udall said.

She might have been speaking in some obscure dialect from a foreign land. Henry Udall heard the words but understood nothing. He gestured impatiently with his cane. "We'll talk about it later. Some other time. Can't you see that I'm . . . ?"

A ghostly scarecrow figure moved up behind Henry Udall. "Matter of fact," Tinkle drawled wearily, rosy firelight playing on his blackened face, "I used to wonder about it myself. Did you kill Hagle and Matthews?"

Udall's voice rose almost to screaming pitch. "Has everyone gone insane! Of course I didn't kill them!"

"Or have it done?"

He hesitated for just a moment. "No!" But that instant of silence had been the truthful answer. Now they knew. They didn't know what, if anything, to do about it. But they knew.

Giles Udall lurched toward them out of the smoke. "Has anybody seen that saloon woman?"

Emily and Tinkle and Henry Udall stood like statues. At last Henry Udall was just beginning to understand his daughter. Perhaps for the first time he saw her as a woman and not merely a bearer of his name. What a drunkard like Tinkle might think did not affect him in any way. His daughter was a different matter. Emily had hurt him, and he could not understand the reason for it. He died without understanding it.

In later times Richter thought about it often, but it was impossible to guess what might have been in Cleet's mind at the moment he squeezed the trigger. Possibly he held some secret grudge against Udall. Or perhaps, to Cleet, Udall represented authority, and he was the type to strike blindly at any and all authority. But most likely it was a simple act of pleasure— Richter remembered the grin of satisfaction on the gunhand's face when he had shot the unsuspecting vaquero out of his saddle. At any rate Cleet was no longer a gunhand with no actual killings to his credit, except for Mexicans, which didn't count. He could cut his first notch now, a big one. He had killed a Udall.

To Richter it was like something out of an alcoholic dream. Henry Udall staggered back under the impact of the bullet. His tall hat fell off and rolled in the gravel. He dropped his cane and collapsed. An old man, as dead as a Comanche cave mummy.

Emily Udall did not move except to step to one side as her father fell, as if to avoid soiling her dress with blood. Giles Udall dived at his sister and knocked her off her feet. Tinkle stared for an instant into the smoke, tears cutting white gullies in his blackened cheeks.

Richter had Giles in his sights, but now he shifted and laid on Tinkle. The moment seemed to freeze. His finger was hard on the trigger. The blade sight found the exact center of Tinkle's left shirt pocket. Then he realized that Tinkle wasn't armed. He didn't know why that should make a difference, but it did. A kind of sick panic came in Tinkle's face. He darted first to one side, then to the other, and Richter led him with deadly expertness back and forth in the swirling smoke. He could not squeeze the trigger.

But unarmed men were not privileged where Cleet was concerned. The revolver bellowed a second time. With cool deliberateness the gun-hand aimed at Tinkle's stomach, and the bullet went where it was aimed. Tinkle's hands grabbed his middle. The lanky figure seemed to break in half.

An unreasoning fury swept over Richter. He scrambled to the near side of the chopping block and brought his rifle to bear on Cleet's position. But Cleet had wisely moved to the far side of the shed and out of sight. Richter saw that his hands were trembling. His throat was constricted and the sweat on his face was clammy and cold. He cursed himself for a fool for tying up with a killer like Cleet in the first place.

Little by little, he made himself settle down and take a more reasonable view. Before this affair was over he might be grateful for Cleet's special knack for murder.

Two horses charged out of the whirling pink smoke, and Cleet made his first mistake. He fired without being sure of his target. Drago dumped out of the saddle on one side, Pedro on the other. They squirmed and scuttled and crawled amidst the clutter of the yard, and seemed to melt into the ground and disappear.

"Drago! Pedro!" Giles Udall's voice was shrill with rage. "They're over there, back of the harness shed. It must be Richter. Double bounty to the man that kills him!"

Drago and Pedro made a deadly team. They slithered like gray snakes in a fog. Richter fired twice but knew that he had succeeded only in showing his position. They didn't burn a cartridge until they were exactly where they wanted to be. When they had the shed in a perfect and deadly crossfire, then they would go to work. To add more weight to their end of the scales, the four vaqueros from Glory were racing up the slope to take a hand.

Drago and Pedro were set. A rifle slug slammed straight through the shed, and splinters flew in Richter's face. Jessie Marchand gasped.

Richter shot a look at the huddled figure. "You all right?"

". . . Yes."

Cleet was firing regularly now, and Richter thought he heard a growing panic in the erratic bursts. This was some different, he thought, from shooting unarmed men from cover.

Now the vaqueros had moved in and were beginning to pepper the shed with rifle fire. From somewhere in the confusion Giles Udall shouted something in Spanish. Richter understood what it was all about when one of the vaqueros darted forward and lobbed a piece of the burning shed at their position. There wasn't enough fire already, they wanted to burn this harness shed down on top of them!

Richter fired into the heart of the torch the instant it left the vaquero's hands. The man yelled, and reeled back into the smoke. The burning plank hadn't reached the shed, but it lay in front of it throwing the area in a harsh red light, which was almost as bad.

In the meantime Drago and his sidekick were methodically shooting the shed to pieces. But Giles Udall was wild with grief and rage. Their way wasn't fast enough to suit him. "Move closer!" he kept yelling. "Closer! Don't let them get away!"

Drago and Pedro, good, obedient gunhands, were not ones to shirk when they had to earn their fighting pay. They moved in closer.

There was a yell of pain from the far side of the shed. Richter lay rigidly as Cleet screamed and kicked and writhed in the gravel and weeds. It couldn't have lasted more than a few seconds. It seemed a long time. "Charge the shed!" Giles Udall yelled. Over to Richter's right he studied a rude triangle of stacked firewood. Easy enough, he thought, to hide behind a few ricks of wood and order your boys to charge into rifle fire.

Apparently, the two gunhands, as well as the vaqueros, were thinking along the same line. Nobody moved. They crouched behind rocks, or clumps of weeds, or some other sort of makeshift breastworks, coughing and wheezing under the cover of ground-hugging smoke.

Giles screamed, "Did you hear me!"

To Richter's surprise he stood up in full view, backlighted by the fires that were slowly eating their way toward the east wall. He broke suddenly from the woodpile and rushed the shed. That did it. Drago and two of the vaqueros rushed in from on Richter's blind side. Pedro and another vaquero loomed in the middleground.

Farther to Richter's right Giles rushed toward

him, firing his .45 as he ran. Richter took one deep breath and held it. There was nothing he could do about Drago and the two vaqueros, he couldn't even see them. He took stock quickly. Giles, he judged, led Pedro by several steps. He shot Giles. Quickly, efficiently. Then he turned the rifle on Pedro. The Mexican dropped in his tracks beside the burning plank.

The vaquero who had been trailing Pedro lost heart. Suddenly the bounty didn't seem so desirable. Not worth dying for, anyway. He wheeled and raced back into the smoke, and Richter let him go. He was vaguely surprised to find that he was still alive. He had expected Drago to appear before now and settle things. Then he saw Jessie Marchand kneeling at the corner of the shed, clutching Cleet's .45 in both hands and firing into the rolling smoke. Now he knew why Drago hadn't come up on his blind side to finish things off.

Richter left his place behind the chopping block and scrambled for the shed. Jessie continued to fire until the hammer snapped on an empty cartridge. Richter slipped the rifle muzzle around the corner and fired once to let Drago know they were still in business.

"Where are they?"

She shook her head. "I don't know." Her face was dirty white in that eerie light that sifted through the smoke. "I heard them. Then I found the pistol. There were three of them—I think they backed off toward the corral."

Richter could just see the shadowy outline of the corral.

"Do you think they'll try again?" she asked.

"I don't know. The old man's done for. Giles too, I think. And Pedro. It wouldn't be much trouble for Drago and the Mex hands to finish us off, now that Drago's free to run the show his own way."

"Why don't they do it?"

Drago himself answered the question. His voice was muffled and strangely disembodied as he called through that curtain of choking smoke.

"Miss Emily, you hear me? Looks like Giles went and got hisself killed. Pedro too." He coughed several times. "Looks like you're the boss now. What you want us to do?"

Jessie Marchand held Richter's arm with cold, stiff fingers. There in the dancing firelight they could see the bodies of Emily's father and brother. All she had to do was give Drago the word, and he would fill her cup of vengeance. But from behind the woodpile where she was hiding, there came no sound.

"What about the bounty, Miss Emily?" Drago called. "Is it still good, like your pa wanted it?"

Richter held his breath. In his mind he could see Drago and the vaqueros flanking them and shooting them to pieces at their leisure. There was a chance that they might do it just for the hell of it, because of Pedro. On the other hand, friendship didn't count for much with gunhands. Cleet hadn't done much grieving over Max.

"Miss Emily . . ." Drago sounded worried. He could see all that money sifting through his fingers.

An arid silence gripped that rocky slope. Then Emily Udall rose up behind the stacked wood. She walked slowly into the smoke and shifting light and she stood for a moment over the bodies of her men. "Drago," she said at last, "get some hands together. Get the laborers that are fighting the fire and bring them up here."

"The *bounty,* Miss Emily!" the gunhand pleaded.

She turned to face away from the drifting smoke and coughed. "There is no bounty. Not any more."

"But your pa!"

"My father's dead. My brother's dead. Bring up the hands; I want to start the graves."

Richter felt Jessie Marchand tremble. He was holding her in one arm.

Drago said bitterly, "Your pa promised! Anyhow, we can't take the workers off the fire. The whole basin'll go up!"

She turned and peered for a moment into the smoke, as if she were looking at the basin for the last time, and hating it. "There will be extra pay for gravedigging," she said, "but not for killing."

"Miss Emily," Drago tried for one last time. "The whole basin'll go."

"Let it go," she said, as if the thought pleased her. ". . . Let it go."

Drago was a realist; if loaves were not to be had, he would settle for crumbs. By morning the graves were finished. In the first hour of dawn the burying was done and the graves refilled. All of it, from beginning to end, was done in grim silence.

By some minor miracle a shifting wind had driven the fire upon itself and killed it, but the dirty smoke lay over the basin like some gigantic shroud. Richter was eager to put the place behind him; he was sick of it, and of the people in it, and besides that his shoulder was beginning to pain him.

But Jessie Marchand would not leave yet. She had the notion that she and Emily Udall had found something in common, and she had the further ridiculous notion that a saloon girl could be of some comfort to a Udall. Richter could have told her, but she wouldn't have listened. He could simply have walked away, which would have been smarter, and considered himself lucky just to be alive.

He discovered that he could not do that either. In a way it was due to Jessie Marchand that he was still alive, and somehow he could not make himself leave her now. And there was still another reason. Tinkle, shot in the stomach by Cleet's .45, had taken a long time dying.

He had lasted until the first hard light of dawn, and most of the time Richter had been with him. Drago and the vaqueros lost all interest in the war now that the prospect of quick riches no longer existed.

Drago was ramrodding the gravedigging detail with the same cool efficiency that he would have engineered Richter's murder. Digging in that rocky earth was slow going, but the gunhand kept the work moving smoothly and the flinty ring of shovels and pick axes formed an uninterrupted clamor in the night.

Jessie Marchand still clutched to Richter's arm, and Richter held determinedly to his rifle, just in case the war suddenly came to life again. But Drago only gave him a coldly curious glance and said, "Mark this day down, Richter. You'll never know a luckier one."

Richter believed him completely.

In the center of the half circle of fire Emily Udall sat in one of those dark, massive chairs that one of the hands had brought from the house. She made a chilling and bizarre figure at the heart of a bizarre scene. Off to one side lay the row of dead waiting for the grave. Emily Udall did not look in that direction. Nearby a vaquero with a wounded arm hunkered on the ground, rocking back and forth and moaning. She turned angrily and snapped something at him in his own language. The moaning stopped.

Richter stared at the row of dead. During the war—the real war—he had seen death, of course. Much worse than this. But that had been organized, almost sanctified slaughter, and was to be expected. This was different.

Jessie Marchand released Richter's arm and started hesitantly toward Emily Udall.

Richter said, "Let her be. She won't take kindly to anything you say, and she might just decide to restart the shootin'."

Jessie shook her head stubbornly. There had been a moment, in the house, when she had seen with frightening clarity into the darkest corners of Emily Udall's thoughts. Now, with so much misery all around her, there seemed that there must be something she could do.

Emily sat bolt upright staring into swirling smoke, and did not look around when Jessie Marchand approached her.

"Miss Udall . . ."

Still she did not move.

"Miss Udall, I know how you must feel . . ."

In no way did Emily Udall acknowledge her presence.

"I mean, there must be something I could do."

Emily sat for a moment, her face waxy, her

eyes dull. At last she turned her head and looked at Jessie Marchand. "How," she asked with the cutting edge of a razor, "could you possibly know what I feel? And what could a border-town doxie possibly do for a Udall?"

Jessie Marchand fell back as if a bullet had torn through her middle. Richter had looked on in grim silence. He had known for a long time that there was no such a thing as a tame wolf, but it was something that Jessie had to learn for herself.

Richter stared past the fire to that dark wall of rock down where Cabot was no doubt watching all this and wondering what it was about. He gestured to Jessie Marchand who was pale with shock.

"Over there's some horses," he said, nodding toward the corral. "Time we got out of here. I don't trust Drago to stay this peaceful forever—and I trust a Udall even less. With any luck we can make it to Cabot, and maybe over the wall, by sunup."

He was gazing bleakly at the row of dead that Drago, on a whim, had laid out like fenceposts. As Richter looked, one of the corpses began to groan.

An icy finger moved up Richter's back. He moved forward and gingerly inspected the dead faces. He bent over Tinkle, and Tinkle looked back at him with eyes that were full of pain and sadness.

"Drago!" Richter shouted angrily. "This man's alive!"

The gunhand was totally uninterested. "He won't be by the time we get his grave finished."

And Drago was right, of course. Richter knew it and Tinkle knew it. "I forget," Tinkle whispered. "Was it your notion or was it mine, startin' a cow operation here in the basin?"

Richter knelt beside him. "Mine, I guess."

"It was a rotten notion," Tinkle sighed. "You got any whiskey?"

Richter shook his head.

Tinkle smiled faintly, "Just as well. I'm gutshot. Couldn't hold it, anyhow." He closed his eyes, quietly gathering the frayed ends of his strength. "Sorry, Richter," he said at last. "About Hagle. Matthews. You. A lot of things."

Richter wanted to hate him. He couldn't. "Don't talk," he said. "Just lay quiet and rest."

With great effort Tinkle moved his head from one side to the other. "Got to talk. Feel in my coat pocket. Inside."

In the pocket Richter found a folded paper. By the flickering light he could make out the name of a bank in El Paso, but that was all. "Show that to the president of the bank. He'll give you some papers I put in his vault. Deed to a piece of land out there, outside the basin."

Richter was puzzled. There was precious little on the other side of the basin except gravel and cactus and thornbrush. "What about it?"

Tinkle's thin lips curved in the faintest of smiles. "Under that land is the underground stream that rises in the gravel bed here in the basin. You could plant a few kegs of blastin' powder and blow it to Kingdom come. Dry the basin up like a bone."

"Why would I want to do that?"

"Don't have to do it. Just be able to, if you take the notion. Only way to keep the Udalls in line." He sighed wearily. "How you think I managed to stay alive all this time? Udalls had to keep me in good health till they figgered a way to get that deed."

Richter looked in wonder at that dry face pinched with pain. The other partners had always known that Tinkle was the smart one. Smart with figures, smart about people. But, behind those weakish eyes, Richter had never expected to find this kind of animal-like cunning. "You can't handle the Udalls any other way," Tinkle said in a sighing whisper. "You got to fight them by their own rules."

Even if it meant getting your friends killed? But Richter didn't say it.

"Richter . . ."

"I'm here."

"My insides're on fire. I ain't goin' to last long."

"Stop talkin' and get some rest. You'll be fine."

Tinkle smiled his death's head smile. "You're tough, Richter. Tougher than any of us. With that deed in your pocket you can beat the Udalls."

"The Udalls're dead, Tinkle. There ain't anybody left but Emily."

But Tinkle didn't hear. He was too busy with his own elusive thoughts. "I failed, like Hagle and Matthews, because of Emily. I wanted to get the basin back, and make things right with you . . . But I never got around to it."

Richter knew that he was lying. He said nothing.

Tinkle stared unblinkingly at the shrouded sky. Richter felt as old as the dark mountains that surrounded them. What had been between himself and Tinkle was now thoroughly dead; not even hate had survived.

"Richter . . ."

"Yes."

"If worst comes to worst, blow it up. Destroy the water. It's the only way you can beat the Udalls."

"I'll think about it," Richter said.

"It's the only way," Tinkle said again in a voice so weak that it was hardly a sound at all.

Richter waited, saying nothing, feeling nothing. After what must have been a long while Jessie Marchand touched his shoulder and said, "He's dead, Richter. He's been dead for some time now."

Richter and Jessie Marchand rode away from the Udall headquarters on two Udall horses, leading a third for Cabot. By the time they reached him the Ranger was feverish and mean as a copperhead.

"Right good of you," he said with dripping sarcasm, "to oblige me by ridin' this way again."

"How's the leg?" Richter asked.

"Burnin' like a pitch barrel!" He had several well-thought-out observations to make on the way things had been bungled from start to finish, thanks to Richter. Richter listened for a while, and then he said, "That's enough."

He said it so coldly and meant it so definitely that Cabot broke off in the middle of a profanity. "That bad?" he asked.

"Bad enough."

"What damn fool started that fire? The whole basin could of gone up."

Richter tightened the binding on the Ranger's leg. "I started it. It seemed like a good idea at the time."

"All right," Cabot said impatiently, "let's hear about it."

"Later."

Cabot flared. "Now!"

Richter stood and looked at him for a steady half minute. "Later," he said again. This time Cabot let him have his way.

• • •

Several long and often painful hours lay between the time the three of them left the basin and the time they raised the familiar mud hut of Mama Sam's. By that time Richter had told his story. But he did not tell about his final conversation with Tinkle.

Richter reined up in sight of the hut. "You aim to lay over here on your way to El Paso?"

Cabot nodded, his face flushed, his eyes swimming with fever.

"Any reason I have to go on to El Paso with you?" Richter asked.

The Ranger shook his head, glad enough to have him off his hands. Jessie Marchand stared straight ahead. Cabot looked at her and touched his hatbrim. "I'm afraid I put you to a lot of trouble . . ."

"It wasn't any trouble," she said, almost wistfully.

Cabot looked at her, then at Richter. He nodded curtly and rode off toward Mama Sam's.

Richter slumped in his saddle. Beyond those high Chanattes four soldiers had thought to build an empire. Now the empire was dead, as well as three of the soldiers and several others.

"What," Jessie Marchand asked at last, "are you going to do about the deed?"

"I don't know." His mind was blank. He

couldn't seem to think past the gnawing void in his gut.

"If Emily Udall tries to keep the basin will you destroy the water?"

". . . Maybe. Right now it doesn't seem all that important."

She smiled fleetingly. "Adios, Richter."

Something like alarm appeared in his eyes. "Where you headed?"

She lifted one shoulder—the saloon girl shrug. "Back to Kopec's."

Richter took his time answering. "No," he said at last, as though he had reached the decision after much careful consideration. "Not Kopec's."

"Then some other place. They're all the same."

Richter didn't seem to hear her. "I don't think I want any more of that basin. But I don't see much sense ruinin' it for somebody else. If Emily Udall don't want my part of it—and I don't expect she does—most likely we can find some cowman to take it over. Get enough out of it, anyhow, to stake us somewheres else."

That, apparently, was as plain as he was capable of making it. Jessie Marchand asked in a thin voice, ". . . We?"

"Why not? We wouldn't make the worst lookin' team I ever saw." He shot her a narrow look. "Of course, if you *want* to go back to Kopec's . . ."

"No. I don't want that." Her eyes were wide.

It seemed that they had gone as far as words

could take them. Suddenly she laughed. It was a soft, tired sound, with no sadness in it.

Richter looked at her for several seconds, really looked at her, as he had done only once or twice before. He was not particularly surprised to find that what he saw he liked.

Books are produced in the United States using U.S.-based materials

Books are printed using a revolutionary new process called THINKtech™ that lowers energy usage by 70% and increases overall quality

Books are durable and flexible because of smythe-sewing

Paper is sourced using environmentally responsible foresting methods and the paper is acid-free

Center Point Large Print
600 Brooks Road / PO Box 1
Thorndike, ME 04986-0001 USA

(207) 568-3717

US & Canada:
1 800 929-9108
www.centerpointlargeprint.com